Margaret Davis Burton

The Woman Who Battled for the Boys in Blue

Mother Bickerdyke - Her Life and Labors for the Relief of our Soldiers

Margaret Davis Burton

The Woman Who Battled for the Boys in Blue
Mother Bickerdyke - Her Life and Labors for the Relief of our Soldiers

ISBN/EAN: 9783337093754

Printed in Europe, USA, Canada, Australia, Japan

Cover: Foto ©Raphael Reischuk / pixelio.de

More available books at **www.hansebooks.com**

THE WOMAN WHO BATTLED FOR THE BOYS IN BLUE.

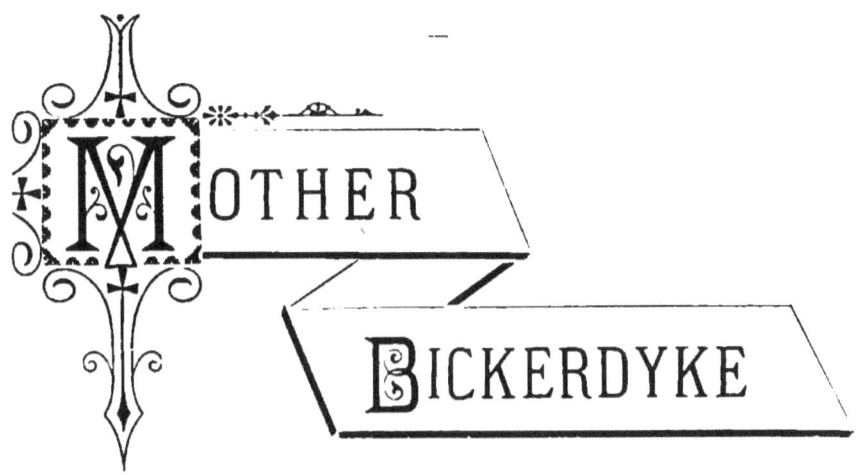

MOTHER BICKERDYKE

Her Life and Labors for the Relief of Our Soldiers. Sketches of Battle Scenes and Incidents of the Sanitary Service.

WRITTEN BY

MARGARET B. DAVIS.

PUBLISHED FOR THE BENEFIT OF M. A. BICKERDYKE.

SAN FRANCISCO, CAL.:
PRINTED AND SOLD BY A. T. DEWEY.
Office of the Fraternal Record.
1886.

PACIFIC PRESS PUBLISHING HOUSE.

PRINTERS, ELECTROTYPERS AND BINDERS,

OAKLAND AND SAN FRANCISCO.

To the Soldiers

Who Preserved the Integrity & American Republic

BY THEIR COURAGE AND PATRIOTISM,

Through Toil, Sickness, Wounds and Death,

THIS BOOK IS DEDICATED.

PREFATORY.

—— o ——

ISTORY has usually been written in the glare of battle-fields, to extol the name of kings and heroes, while the little rills from the heart that flowed into the abodes of want and wretchedness, stanching bleeding wounds and drying the falling tear, have been too often overlooked. The world is not rich enough to neglect the touching story of Florence Nightingale in the Crimea, or of the hundreds of Florence Nightingales whose sweet and tender ministries softened the grim features of the civil war. And no one of that host of tender-hearted women who went out under the auspices of the Sanitary or Christian Commission rendered more valuable service in the hospitals than Mary A. Bickerdyke. Such is the united testimony of those great soldiers, Grant, Sherman, Logan, Pope, and Miller, all of whom knew her well. But she needs no testimonials, for her name and noble deeds are still fragrant in the memory of the officers and soldiers of the Western armies.

But memory is frail, the present generation will soon pass away, while the heroic deeds of this remarkable woman are too precious to go out in oblivion. It has been a work of pleasure and gratification on the part of the publisher to secure the facts and thrilling incidents of this noble life, and crystallize them into a permanent shape for the example and inspiration of future generations.

This book has been prepared and published specially for her benefit. For years her heroic labors received no recognition from a Government that has been liberal in rewarding its soldiers. This may have been partly owing to that shrinking diffidence that cared not to have its merits measured in dollars and cents. True worth is ever modest and retiring. It is a flower that loves the shade. Still, the laborer is worthy of his reward, and some friends a short time ago secured for her a pension from the Government, a mere pittance, wholly insufficient to furnish a reasonable support, now that the infirmities of age have made her unable longer to care for herself. Surely the soldiers she loved so well, the ladies of the Relief Corps, and a patriotic public, will not forget her now. Every one who buys this little volume will not only have a souvenir of a noble woman, but the satisfaction of knowing that they have helped to brighten the few remaining years of one who gave her best energies in relieving the sick, consoling the dying, and transmitting to the homes of the living the last words of their brave dead.

CONTENTS.

CHAPTER I.

CHAPTER II.

CHAPTER III.

CHAPTER IV.

CHAPTER V.

CHAPTER VI.

CHAPTER VII.

Mother Bickerdyke.

CHAPTER I.

RS. MARY A. BICKERDYKE is noted throughout the length and breadth of our country for her success as a soldiers' nurse in the War of the Rebellion. Her motherly kindness to her charges made her name among them synonymous with all that is tender and grand in motherhood; and for this reason she became widely known as Mother Bickerdyke. The appellation suits her well. She bears it as a general does his title; and her individuality gives to it a refinement which those who are not acquainted with her may fail to understand.

Mars, that crimson torch of the war god, which follows the track of the sun, must have burned over her

birthplace when she came to earth, if there is any
truth in the astrologer's erudition; for she is one who
might have faced dangers, such as she has braved,
with the purpose of destroying, and made as many
wounds as she has soothed, if Providence had not set
beneath her breastplate that matchless jewel, a mother's heart. This places in her hand a vial of balm instead of a sword, and causes her to look upon the
soldier with the eyes of a mother instead of those of
an enemy. Therefore in every bosom where sentiments of patriotism and of fraternal love are cherished,
the name of "Mother Bickerdyke" awakens feelings of
friendship. Her life is marked by events of thrilling
interest, and characterized by practical work strangely
mingled with romantic incidents.

In that part of San Francisco called the Mission
"Mother Bickerdyke" now makes her home. She
was invited to the Pacific Coast, as so many others
have been, by the balmy climate, and by the fortune
which seems to those of every other land beckon-
ing to them with smiles. From the scene of her
youth and labors, and from the homes of her children, she came to begin a new work alone, her
only aids being great courage, and the title by which
she is distinguished in relation to the many brave
men who fought in the War of the Rebellion. Still,
this title, which might become, if possessed by one dif-
ferently constituted, the " open sesame " to all that is
desirable in wealth or fame, is, in her hands, only
the wine and oil of the good Samaritan flowing for
her soldier boys.

In all the changeful scenes which her special personal qualities predestined her to pass through, she
has found none more fair and peaceful than those
which surround her in the present. Her home is in
the upper part of a house, from the windows of which
may be seen the waving outlines of the Potrero hills,
a gleam of the bay to the eastward, and, all about,
the numberless dwellings that help to form the city.
The sound of the ancient Mission Church bells may
often be heard in her quiet, orderly chambers. At
morning and evening they ring as of yore, when
the Mission fathers first heard them, over one hundred years ago. This church is only a few blocks
away, and now those priests are sleeping beneath the
myrtles and mossy stones, in the little cemetery that
half encircles its adobe walls, which are seamed with
age. Here the streets are rather quiet, and neither
ostentatious wealth nor squalid poverty appear to
disturb the current of humanity. The world of toil
and trade, and the stirring elements that excite war,
seem shut away from this sunny, sheltered spot. It
is favored with monuments of the past which speak,
to an imaginative mind, of earlier scenes that were
looked upon by the first of our own race, who made
their homes in this new land. The flocks and herds
of the Mission Dolores grazed upon these grassy
slopes, over which the soft blue of heaven seems
bending low and tenderly. Here and there remains
some crumbling habitation in which the Indian con-
verts were sheltered long before the discovery of gold.
They built those abodes with their own dark hands;

while the priests directed them with the patience and
sternness their barbarous, yet submissive, minds demanded. How full of wonder must have been the
children of the woods, to see the new church in the
freshness of its gilded shrines and bright paintings,
so surprising and delightful to their savage fondness
for color! The ceremonies of dedicating the tem-
ple to its patron, St. Francis, whom they were taught
to call San Francisco in the sweet Spanish tongue,
and the inscription upon the arch encircling the
altar, must have been almost incomprehensible to
them. The Mission fathers seemed to have thought
that they could understand fear more readily than
love. The words selected for their eyes, whenever
they should come to worship, were, " How terrible is
this place! This is none other but the house of God,
and the gate of Heaven."

These primitive scenes have passed away entirely,
and the new people, who claim the soil, have appropriated the Mission Dolores and its lands to their own
purposes. Still its associations appear to forbid any
but those who desire peaceful homes and quiet pursuits, from coming to mar the pleasant picture.
Among the modern dwellings stands the old church,
with its stout, white pillars in front, and its long, narrow roof of tiles swaying with the weight of years.
The wise Mission fathers selected this locality because
it is particularly favored by nature Flowers bloom
in the garden plots perpetually, and the fogs, that so
often rise from the ocean, are kept out by the hills that
also shelter this place from the winds. Time seems

trying to cheat mortals into the belief that the sands in his glass have ceased running; and insidiously invites age to an appropriate season of repose before the twilight hours of life have lost the glow of its sunbeams.

But "Mother Bickerdyke" heeds no such allurements. For years she has been seen frequently in the narrow doorway of her home, with bonnet and wrap donned ready to proceed into the realms of business. Without fear or special company, she travels, in safety, journeys which extend from a trip across the bay, to a tour across the continent. Few who look upon the self-possessed and sensible lady, with her gray hair and plain attire, would perceive the luminous halo shed upon her from the diadem of motherhood gemmed with the stars of patriotism; and which incloses within its shining circle every soldier of the late war as the son of her adoption. But when seen through the glass of her history, she is transformed as if by the magic wand of the fairy godmother that rendered such a wonderful change in Cinderella. Her vestments are white with purity, and brightened with the rose color of romance. They are richly fringed with the pearls of maternal love and duty. Her voice is sweet with the music of hope, and her words are expressions of cheer. Her glance is that of the lioness guarding her young, and wisdom reposes upon her brow. To her sons she is a mother tender to nurse them, strong to help them, and as constant to them in peace as in war.

The work which benefits mankind, and the strength

2

and will which enable one to perform it, impress like an iron mould the form and character; while the bloom an I freshness of youth are worn away by years of toil; so the heroes of the world are usually pictured with lines of care and endurance upon their faces, and with whitened locks beneath the laurels of their glory. After the work of a life-time has been performed, comes the opinion of the world; expressed with much ceremony if the subject is prominent, and in only a passing remark or sigh of pity, if obscure.

Notwithstanding her years, she is lively and energetic. Her figure is erect and portly, and is formed for action and endurance. Back from a broad, well-moulded brow, her gray hair is smoothly brushed, and then twisted, a little carelessly, into an old fashioned coil at the back of her head. Her eyes are of a dark blue color. and look straight at those with whom she speaks; the nose is slightly aquiline; the mouth medium and expressive of firmness; and the well-defined outline of the lower part of her face irregular and characteristic of power. The artist has done well with her picture, the frontispiece. Still the ease and cordiality of her manners, the heartiness and energy of her words, and the mobile expression of her face, are much more indicative of her character than are her form and features, and those can scarcely be portrayed with the pencil.

She is impulsive and full of fire and feeling; a woman designed to do something of note in the world, if circumstances offer an opportunity. All this physical strength and activity of mind could not help but work with energy in any path of life, and the one selected, if individual choice were permitted, would naturally be such as to interest the sympathies.

At the start, a character like this may be compared to a fine ship, built to brave the ocean currents and storms, and worthy to be trusted with lives and treasures. She may sail to well-known harbors of commerce, or to the dangerous polar seas; and her course will be as the hand at the helm directs. This guiding power decides the world-wide difference in the courses that lie before her. Neither pleasure, wealth, nor fame awakened Mother Bickerdyke's aspirations. *Mother!* That is the word which describes the guiding power in this strong, active woman. Motherhood, the crown of feminine perfection, she did not wear as did the beautiful Madonna, bearing in her arms the infant with a spike of lilies in his hand. The divine woman, with her angelic grace and loveliness, seems akin to the invisible spirits of Heaven. This heroine is of a different mould; one in perfect contrast to the saintly picture, although she possesses the true instincts of maternity in such perfection that it suggests the similes while pointing out the difference between them. She is of later centuries, and of another nation and land. American women, and especially those of that part called the Northwest, are nobly represented in her, because she typifies the greater number of the characteristics that distinguish them. But one grace of womanhood is all her own, and shines with a luster unborrowed from her sisters, because few have proved the possession of it in as marked perfection, and none have excelled her.   This is the remarkable depth and strength of her maternal feelings.

She is a Spartan-like mother, possessed of a heart not only ample enough for the children who came to bless her own home; but when her compassion was awakened in behalf of the wounded soldiers who were suffering for their common country, she found room for them all in an ideal sense, and called them, in her whole-souled way, "Our boys" and "My boys."

The grand character here faintly drawn exists among us, and prese ts to our eyes the form of an old lady in her cozy home at the Mission. She is like a great time-worn ship that has weathered a t..ousand gales, and, having carried in safety her priceless freight of life and fortune, is now anchored in the smooth waters of the bay. Yet even such a similitude as this is inadequate to express a perfect comparison; for the peaceful tides of the sheltered haven find her not entirely at ,est. Though nearly seventy years have passed over her head, and many of them have been marked by the cruelest sufferings and losses, she appears ten years younger than most women of her age; and devotes the time which should be a season of perfect enjoyment and repose, to the interests of the men who have been wounded and maimed for the sake of our country, and yet have not received their full and deserved reward.

Mother Bickerdyke, though having done her part so well, still pursues her chosen work with a spirit of independence and unswerving steadfastness of purpose that courts no attention or praise, though she richly deserves both. In a woman's life, it is her public work, and not her private character, that should excite the general interest. Though American women share, in a marked degree, the heritage of freedom which is the common birthright of every citizen of our land, modesty generally keeps their personality within the limits of the social and home circles, however successful may be their labors in behalf of mankind. Still general curiosity demands some recognition as a right, which even Vesta may not deny; and, considering all things, it is better to grant this privilege, since the mere description of a public career often leads to erroneous conclusions on the part of the reader.

For instance, the sketch of Mother Bickerdyke, contained in the book entitled, "Women of the War," although accurate and well written, in so far as its purposes go, conveys the idea that she is a stern, business-like woman, actuated by an uncommonly philanthropic turn of mind. But this falls far short of the reality. Curiosity could never be content until it had lifted the veil from the Turkish beauty's face, and scanned her features. This is what it determines to do with all prominent women, whether they consent or not. If the figure unveiled chances to be admirable, it is praised accordingly; and yet it is as intensely interesting if it affords only materials for criticism. However noble and helpful the work may have been matters not; if the author of it is such as to awaken adverse criticisms, they are meted out to her without stint or mercy. This is scarcely just. It is like pouring nectar from a flagon, and, after sipping the delicious draught, condemning the design and material of the vessel from which it flowed.

To present Mother Bickerdyke's work and character as it is in reality, is a difficult task, though one that is pleasing, on account of its association with so much that is noble and praiseworthy in human nature. Many barriers wall in the simple truth, which it r. quires time and effort to overcome; and as truth in its pristine beauty is fa⁻ more engaging than when embellished by the romancer's art, so wisdom counsels no borrowing of his gilded pen. But the chief difficulty lies in the different state of feeling and of public affairs now, from what existed when Mother Bickerdyke won her distinction. Nearly a quarter of a century has passed since the excitement of war shook the whole country. Willows have grown tall, above the graves that were hollowed out to receive the soldiers who then fell. The agony of parting and suspense, the terrors of battle, the rejoicings of victory, and the lamentations for the dead, are all softened and beautified by the lapse of time.

Even the phase of army life that must be presented is one that may be unrecognized by soldiers themselves, who have served only in times of peace. The tale that fascinates in a prosperous home, is not of prostrate men with ghastly faces, who bleed from undressed wounds; nor yet of dreary hospital wards, where the stillness is broken by groans, and messages from the dying. Ambition and admiration delight to follow the victorious warriors with their glistening bayonets and gorgeous flags, conquering amid the smoke and flame and thunder of the battle. When they march to yet prouder fields, then it is woman's province to weep over the slain and minister to the dying. To follow the mother there must strike a different chord of feeling, and one that is harrowing and sad, as well as tender and melting in its harmony.

Mother Bickerdyke was the daughter of Hiram Ball. She was born in Knox County, Ohio, near the present city of Mt. Vernon, July 19, 1817, which was fifteen years after the admission of that State into the Union, and when those magnificent fields, that now flourish in annual luxuriance of grain, and support numberless homes in the lap of ease and peace, were still interspersed with wild prairies, over which the bison roamed, and where savage tribes pursued their wars. The strongest and most adventurous people of the country were among the settlers in this territory; and there their hardihood was exercised until it became a distinguishing trait of character. A daughter of these dauntless people, and inheriting from them in a marked degree their strength and energy, Mother Bickerdyke was by nature fitted for the scenes in which she became noted. A woman of less robust constitution, or less courageous, though endowed with a spirit of patriotism as lofty, and with sympathies as deep and strong, could never have rendered services so timely and efficient.

Looking backward over the fifty years that intervene between the days of her youth and the present, it may be well to consider her as a young girl. There is profit and pleasure in studying the stages through which such human blossoms are wrought upon by different influences, until they are changed into the fadeless amaranth. She was a maiden of the Hebe type, all freshness and bloom, who loved the open air and sunshine that made her color warm and rich, as though she was always seen in the rosy beams of morning. Her figure was marked by rounded lines that were smooth and firm; and her motions were agile and free with the grace that exuberant strength and spirits give. At art and fashion, with their wiles generally so bewitching, she must have laughed, for she loved liberty in all things. Yet, being a woman, and young and fair, she could not have turned from her mirror without a glance of pride. Her glossy hair was of a light brown shade; and her fine blue eyes merry and sparkling. Her soft cheek, rounded by youth and health, melted with lovely outlines into a neck that was fair and strong as that of a statue.

If she wove bright dreams of what the future might hold for her, it was not as other. girls imagined theirs, while they lived as carelessly as the prairie flowers at their feet. Her very thoughts took the form of actions, and her dreams for the future found expression in present deeds that tended to make them real. Her taste found gratification in practical things, rather than in the ideal. Others might stand in rapture, gazing on emerald seas of prairie land, and wonder at their sublime expanse that seemed limitless, she preferred to make her dwelling cheerful, and her table inviting. Besides the restless energy that made her speech and action changeful as the current of a brook, her disposition to help others, and to share their trials, won for her numberless friends

When she consented to become a wife, the successful suitor was indeed fortunate. He could boast that in all the wide West there could be found no fairer, lovelier bride than his. She made their home bright and cheerful with things designed for comfort and use, rather than for ornament, and saw more beauty in a neat hearth-stone, that reflected a clear, well-replenished blaze, than in decorations which appealed only to an æsthetic taste.

Fairest of all in this home picture, is the young mother so devoted to her darlings. They were ruddy and strong, and filled the house with sounds of childish glee. To such domestic cares was her attention exclusively devoted until the little ones had grown quite mature, and were able to assist her in performing household duties. Then she became a treasure to her friends in the neighborhood, for she was always ready to offer efficient help in the time of need.

These years had stolen from her face and form some of their grace and beauty, but they had developed ˙ her affections and brought to her a rich treasure of experience. Besides she had learned that there was much in the world deserving of censure and condemnation. Her strong feelings sometimes rose like the winds of her native prairies, and spared not the object that offended her sense of honor or right.   In these later years, changes came stealing over her home, as they come to others, with their insidious and resistless influences.   Death had not passed them by without claiming more than one of the dear home treasures.   Still it was the old home indeed, until the funeral prayer and hymn were breathed for the husband and father.

Mrs. Bickerdyke, strong, and keenly sensible of the added duties pressing upon her in consequence of her widowhood, did not give way to overwhelming grief, but bore her loss with fortitude, though her tender heart was pierced with sorrow, as poignant as mortal can experience.   The youngest of her children was then but a few years old, and scarcely out of her arms. Love and duty awakened her energies anew for the sake of the helpless little ones, and life was still full of its absorbing pursuits which she followed with her customary directness and success.   Through all these stages of her existence, which have just been so briefly outlined, she has appeared simply as the faithful wife and mother, beautified by her peculiar talents and virtues, that are for the most part the endowments of nature.   She has done a woman's work in the world, and that cannot be too highly appreciated or praised, though it is only what success demands of every perfect woman's life.   She has fulfilled the mission of womanhood, and in a manner that has won abundant friendship and esteem.   Her strong, willing hand has soothed many a feverish brow, and her hopeful voice brightened the dark hour of death. Her courage and daring have cheered the "weary in well doing," by example; and she has become a pillar in the community to which many eyes have learned to look when counsel or aid is needed.

At this period, the first rumors of war began to ring over the land and engage general attention. Mrs. Bickerdyke, being of a positive and enthusiastic disposition, felt a great interest in the state of her country. Patriotism burned high and strong in her bosom, and her lively words were not spared to inspire in others such sentiments as animated her own.

The winter previous to the breaking out of active hostilities was full of the cruelest suspense and fear. It was a season never to be forgotten, on account of anxiety and hope alternately vibrating, as eagle eyes watched the changing appearance of the war-clouds that were gathering over the nation. As time advanced, the threatened calamity became inevitable, though in every heart, where home and country were held dear, had been cherished the hope that all political differences would be settled in a more amicable way than by means of a great national conflict.

Not until spring had returned with her warm light and showers, brightening the face of nature with vernal blossoms, did the threatening doom become a certainty. On the 12th of April, 1861, Fort Sumter was surrendered by its brave commander, Major Anderson, to General Beauregard, after a terrific bombardment of thirty-four hours' duration. Three days later, President Lincoln issued a call for 75,000 vol-

unteers. State after State was seceding from the
Union, and the highest excitement prevailed, agitating
alike the inhabitants of cities and towns, and the
dwellers in remote rural districts, who came flocking
from their quiet homes to mingle their voices with
the sounds of war.

The youthful, having fewer ties to bind them to the
domestic fireside, and possessing more enthusiastic
and adventurous spirits than those of middle age,
formed the larger number of the volunteers. These
young men, the flower and pride of the country. had
not outgrown the guarding love of their mothers, that
had always pursued them, and yet had awakened in
the fair bosoms of sweethearts and wives those tender emotions natural to their age; and which, though
in times of peace are silken cords, the clarion notes
of war transform into chains stronger than death.
Twice 70,000 hearts followed them with love and
yearnings for their safe return, when they

> "Marched away,
> Looking so handsome, brave, and grand."

From woman's standpo'nt, war is invested with
horrors that are as hard for her to endure as are the
parts which men take for them to bear. Though she
is not called to face the cannon's mouth, and strike
heart-piercing blows upon a fellow-creature, she must
see the husband, on whom she leans, as a vine upon
its support, and the son, whom she cherishes with the
fathomless depth of a mother's love, march bravely
to perils that are doubly terrible to her. The mag-
nitude of woman's patriotism is thus measured by the

greatest tests that it is possible to imagine. How
could they let their darlings go, even for their
country's sake? How could they consent to see no
more the dear, familiar faces, and hear no more the
welcome footsteps and beloved voices in their homes,
knowing all the while that

> Ever onward with the brave,
> Though glory's banners o'er them wave,
>   Death walks with viewless feet,
> That they must wait and watch and pray
> Alone; while trials every day
> Around their loved ones mark the way
>   Till victory is complete.

Still the sacrifice was made in thousands of homes,
before that awful strife was ended. The shadow that
had come to them was changed to a reality, and at
noonday, at twilight, and in the still night hours sad
councils were held in anticipation of the partings
pressing upon them so soon. In those scenes all
human weakness and selfish affection se med absorbed
by the lofty sentiments of patriotism. The grandeur
of the human soul manifested itself in the men and
women who sacrificed every home comfort and personal feeling in response to the call of a duty so sublime.

Did women grieve alone over the forsaken hearth-
stone? Was not the sacrifice as great to the loving
sons and husbands marching away in the magnificent
trappings of war, although their eyes were fixed on
the glories of fame, and their hearts set on victory?

"Do not think my boy felt no sorrow to go," said
a gray-haired mother, while the tears welled into her
eyes. "He was proud and gallant as the captain

himself, but the letters he sent back to us were full of affection and longing for the old place; and his last message, spoken on the bloody field to a comrade, was, 'Tell them at home that I thought of them to the last.'"

When the soldiers were preparing for departure, women had gathered into little circles and made with tact and aptitude the flags that floated in the splendor of all the stars and stripes, over the brave men who had volunteered to die if need be, that not one star should cease to spangle the azure of their standard. The days in which the soldiers departed upon their mission were vividly painted on the memories of those who saw them. Every one realized that never again would that place witness the same vigorous ranks and leaders assembled as now they were. Along the perilous path before them many were sure to fall, yet those scenes were more characterized by hope and faith in the valiant arm than by sorrow. All honor to people so heroic! They are worthy descendants of the men who conquered in the Revolution. With shout and cheer the streets resound while the "boys in blue" pass through them, and the flash of their polished steel and iris-hued banners glitter in the sunlight. Songs of the soaring lark and spring-time's myriad blossoms seem prophesying their predestined victories.

The wistful eyes that watched them depart, through tears, did not cease to weep when the martial music had grown silent in distance; but turned upon the vacant chambers they had left, and became clear only to bend upon some task that might still be a benefit to them. With one accord the women of the country turned their attention to devices for aiding and encouraging the soldiers; and for alleviating the sufferings which they knew would be inevitable. Their love and patriotism did not for a moment permit of their enduring the trials of suspense in idleness and vain regret.

Little more than a vague idea of what would be needed, or the most acceptable, could be entertained by persons who had had no experience in war upon so tremendous a scale. Being generally well read and intelligent, they had gathered from books and periodicals a theoretical knowledge, but this was found to be of little practical value when applied to the present circumstances; and it led to numberless mistakes. Even the most prominent in anticipating and preparing for the consequences of the great battles that were at hand, had no well-defined course of action mapped out for themselves, and in many instances acknowledged this openly. Although they knew not exactly what to do, their feelings demanded expression, and impelled action in some direction that offered a promise of serving those in whom they felt so deep an interest. They did what seemed the most likely to succeed, with a faith and perseverance that could not fail of achieving their object in the end; but in the meantime the tempest was raging, and the land echoed with tales of suffering and want that thrilled every heart.

At this period Mrs. Bickerdyke began the work

which has since made her famous. She was unconscious of the course that lay before her, never entertaining a thought of pursuing any philanthropic work.
Her own life seemed full enough of care and troubles
without adding those of others, although her willing
hands had soothed many a feverish brow, and her
helpful words brightened for many the dark hours of
suffering and pain.

When she had seen the young men march away,
her heart had followed them with all of a mother's
love, as well as a noble woman's patriotism. Her enthusiasm continually increased. Every column in
the daily press was scanned carefully, and every dispatch from the seat of war anxiously considered.
Tales of suffering began to fill the air. Sickness
and neglect prevailed among the disabled soldiers,
and they needed delicate food and tender nursing,
both of which circumstances denied them. Listening to rumors like this, her sympathies were not expressed in words alone, nor was she content to work
blindly as so many did without any assurance of
succeeding in their object. Her mighty soul was
roused to the utmost and began to manifest its remarkable latent powers.

Her constitution and courage rendered the fear of
disease and death an unconceived idea. Toil and
hardship had no terrors for her. Her cheek did not
blanch nor her eyes swim when she heard the thunder of cannon, for her armor of fortitude was in-
vulnerable to shafts like these, although they usually
lacerate feminine sensibilities to the quick. The

thought which filled her was of the brave men fighting valiantly for their country, in spite of shot and shell that showered around them a rain of death. "They are hungry and cold and bleeding, and suffer, with none to minister to their wants," were the words that inspired her to action, while they made others quail and faint. By her deeds, she seemed to say, "My fair sisters, stay you here at the hearth-stone, and prepare bandages and lint for them, while I go to the wars, and with my own hands bind up the wounds of our suffering boys."

CHAPTER II.

THE cold winds that swept over the prairie lands as they lay wrapped in the winter coverlid of snow, were being chained again in their frozen caves. In vain the silvery flakes had sought to mantle the bare trees, for they had been blown from the shivering branches, as fast as they had found a lodgment there. But April came, filling the heavens with sunshine that thrilled, with an impulse of life, the seeds and roots nestling in its bosom. Every leafless twig in the orchards felt the warm kiss of sunbeams, and in response, nature twined them with fresh, rosy blooms, that scented the air with their fragrance. Those sweet fruit blossoms! They are the fairest emblems of hope and promise the world contains. From the town of

(34)

Galesburg, in the bright spring weather, five hundred men had gone to the war, answering, by this heroic action, the first call of our country for defenders. Up through the clear air, smoke wreaths curled from the chimneys, while beneath the roofs all who remained brooded over the nation's trouble. They talked with each other upon this exciting topic, to the exclusion of almost every other subject, and watched anxiously each day for new tidings. But who could be despondent with all the beauties of early spring awakening around them? The unfolding of young leaves and buds invites the mind to hopeful anticipations, and so the girls of Galesburg exchanged with each other sweet confidences concerning their soldier friends and lovers; then they went about their duties with snatches of song on their lips. Young housewives and old mothers prepared the most delicious cakes and sweetmeats, and packed them in strong boxes, with clean linen and other comforts, thinking to send them to their particular loved ones, who were enduring the perils and hardships of civil strife. Mrs. Bickerdyke, in her energetic way, worked for the same purpose, though none of her family had gone with the Galesburg volunteers. Her husband had died two years before, and her sons were so young that they could not be admitted into the army; still her heart was enlisted for her country's welfare, and her hope gilded the edges of every cloud.

She was eminently social in her disposition, and loved to meet people in an informal way; for her object was to learn of what they were thinking and feel-

ing.   Her own ideas were offered freely, and in return
she would not take mere ceremonious commonplaces.
Anything like a taste for gossip was foreign to her
mind.   Whatever she said was for a purpose, and she
had the gift of clothing her thoughts in such quaint,
yet clear expressions, that they struck her hearers
with augmented force, inspiring confidence and gain-
ing candor in return.

During this season the whole town was made
gloomy, by receiving, for burial, the forms of two of
their own volunteers.   One had been the sexton of a
church, and the other a young student, both of whom
the people had known in the pride of youthful manhood; and had seen depart, in the beauty of health
and strength, but a few weeks before.   The usefulness and joy of life they had sacrificed for their land,
and now the dust and ashes of the offering were returned to be placed with their kindred.

The next Sabbath, when the bells were ringing, and
the people, well dressed and decorous, were on their
way to church, they discussed, in subdued tones, the
sad event, and the latest news from the war.

" Mrs. Bickerdyke," said a friend, joining her,
" Major Woodruff has written of the sickness breaking
out among the soldiers at Cairo; perhaps you have
heard already of · their terrible condition.   Some of
them are lying entirely without care or suitable food.
Many are down with typhoid fever, resulting from
hunger and fatigue."

" The Government has not yet been able to provide
relief for them," said another who had joined the

little group. Thus many stood talking earnestly until church time. The services opened with the national hymn; and as the deep notes of the organ and voices pealed in clear strains,

> "My country, 'tis of thee,
> Sweet land of liberty,
> Of thee I sing,"

The truth was brought forcibly home to every heart, how deeply they did

> "Love thy rocks and rills,
> Thy woods and templed hills,"

And how they had already proved that love by their sacrifices. Then the minister, Dr. Beecher, told them that his heart was too much in the cause of their land to allow him to do anything but prepare to relieve he suffering soldiers. His words were answered by every member with deep sympathy, and consequently church service was discontinued, in order that they might do the will of Heaven by performing the duties their leader pointed out to them.

They all went to work eagerly, and with a definite purpose. Now their contributions were not only delicacies, but many a motherly heart recalled what her own family had required in sickness, and sent things of a like nature to those who were sick, and far away from loving care. Pity and charity may have influenced these noble workers, but the mainspring of their zeal was love and patriotism, so blended as to form one overpowering sentiment. In such a company, the timid or negative in disposition naturally look to the strong and positive for direction and help. The majority of women bend like the willow, to let the storm pass over them; and when one braves it with unflinching courage and strength, they rally around her as if she were their captain.

"How fortunate the sick men at Cairo would be if you could go down to them, Mrs. Bickerdyke," said one. "You have had experience in such work and are so strong and encouraging," added another.

"Surely all these things must go in charge of one or more of us, so let us elect delegates," a lady among them suggested; and accordingly those who were best fitted to superintend the distribution of their gifts, and who could best be spared from home duties, were chosen. By Monday afternoon, a number of car loads ready for shipment were placed in their charge. Among them none looked with more pleasure or confidence upon their duties than Mrs. Bickerdyke. Her blue eyes beamed with enthusiasm, as she discussed plans with her friends. Over the broad prairie lands sped the train, carrying all this precious freight. The level stretches that met the blue horizon far away were green as emeralds with crisp young verdure expanding in the sunlight; and across this beautiful plair Mrs. Bickerdyke gave a parting glance at the fair homes of Galesburg, and started upon her noble, voluntary mission.

When they arrived at Cairo, with their offerings of comfort and cheer, Mrs. Bickerdyke said in her practical way, "The greatest blessing that could be bestowed upon the poor, brave boys would be to give them good nursing and good housekeeping." What a change took place in their miserable condition!

Order was restored around them, and comfort gained supremacy over pain. Their wards were transformed from close, uncleanly places of suffering to wholesome, airy chambers that invited the return of health. The tempting food Mrs. Bickerdyke gave them was accepted with smiles that had long been absent from their thin, wan faces; and in return for her offerings, she was blessed by those whom she had comforted. She remained with them during that long summer, and although she heard the news of battles throughout the land, her heart was here, faithfully bent upon the one duty that seemed paramount,—the ministering to sufferers who were at hand. Even when the Confederate forces were gathering at Belmont, only a short distance down the broad Mississippi, she remained at her post, scarcely heeding them: But when later Colonel Ulysses S. Grant, in command of three thousand Illinois troops, passed through Cairo, she beheld them with interest and pride.

"They will need me at Belmont after the battle," may have been her thought, as she looked at the strong men in their dusty uniforms, marching with firm tread to the field; and she must have shuddered to imagine how pale and changed some of them would be when she should behold them again. They seemed to follow their leader with only the thought of triumph.

After this battle took place, Mrs. Bickerdyke was assigned to the field hospitals. Here in the chill November weather, the wounded men could only be exposed to sufferings and death more cruel than that showered upon them by the opposing forces; so they were removed, as soon as possible, to floating hospitals.

The tide of war sweeping onward, marking its course by a trail of crimson, was slightly stayed by the stormy winter months. While the snow mantled the earth with robes of vestal purity, men seemed loath to stain it with each other's blood. The experience of the last year had made the necessity of providing better care for those who fell wounded in battle, and for the sick, apparent. Many efforts to this end were being made.

In June, 1861, the Secretary of War issued an order appointing a Committee of Inquiry and Advice, in respect to the sanitary interests of the United States forces. The men selected for this duty met in Washington and organized the United States Sanitary Commission. This body established co-workers and agents in the principal cities, at a distance where they could be of the greatest advantage in forming branches to aid in the great sanitary work. During the fall a powerful auxiliary branch was organized in Chicago. Afterward, this assumed even greater proportions than any of the numerous others; and besides, became a reservoir to receive and forward, to the best advantage, the important contributions sent to the army by different individuals, and by aid societies. When the Union forces were preparing to advance into the territory occupied by the Confederates, Dr. Aigner, a member of the United States Sanitary Commission, projected the plan of establishing a line of floating hospitals, that should be kept near the gun-boats upon the Southern waters. This idea met with approval, and the first of these sanitary steamers was set afloat in the Mississippi. It proved to be a success and was soon joined by others. Large supplies of Government stores were obtained, and surgeons and nurses were secured for the soldiers. Thus it was that when the campaign of 1862 opened, the hands of Liberty were filled with balm for healing those who should suffer in her cause.

The eyes of the warrior, looking southward, rested upon Fort Henry, as a Confederate stronghold to be taken; and accordingly Grant moved forward with his soldiers while a fleet of gun-boats went up the Cumberland, to act in concert with the land forces. The snows and heavy rains of February drenched the ground, as the invading army proceeded, and the flotilla made way with greater speed against the swollen volume of the river. Before Grant and his men had time to begin operations, Commodore Foote compelled the Confederates to evacuate the fort, most of the prisoners escaping to Donelson.

Among several nurses and surgeons of the army, Mrs. Bickerdyke was here, rejoicing over the good fortune of the victors, with more than patriotic feelings, since so few men had been wounded. Now her willing hands were free from duty, so she found time to view the scenes around her with an unpreoccupied mind. She stood looking out through the chill air of the winter night at the camp-fires of Grant's army. The dark figures of the soldiers moved to and fro against the ruddy lights, that revealed with flickering gleams their surroundings, and the stars above appeared like white diamond points in contrast. The glowing flames were cheerful to the men who were weary with marching, and perhaps in the embers some soldier pictured his far-away home and treasures, while he thought of the morrow which would find him among the ranks starting to besiege another stronghold; and that promised not to be so easily taken as the one captured to-day. But the warm blaze caused comrades to talk of their friends and loved ones, and to encourage each other with prospects of future triumphs, until sleep in mercy made them forget their present perils. To Mrs. Bickerdyke this was an impressive scene, and one that remained in her memory ever after.

The next morning the troops started for Fort Donelson, leaving their overcoats and all unnecessary things behind them. A fair blue sky arched above, and they went as gaily as if to a banquet. Now their aim was victory, and the thought of failure thrilled them with redoubled determination to take the fort. The gun-boats hastened, by way of the river, to the point of attack. In the meantime, the world looked on with anxious eyes, watching their proceedings. Many a heart ached with dread and suspense every hour during that severe struggle; while the soldiers who took part in it suffered untold agonies. The weather changed suddenly, and winter blew upon the unprotected ranks with piercing winds, and rain, and snow. For three days the fight lasted; and the assailing forces endured hunger and cold,

lying down at night exhausted upon the bare, wet
earth, and arising at dawn, unrefreshed, to recom-
mence the terrible contest. Shot and shell poured
into the bright waters of the Tennessee, and the
helpful gun-boats were driven back with heavy losses;
but Grant's determined men, strong in faith and
dauntless in courage, kept up the siege until the fort
surrendered. The great North was filled with rejoicing, which was loudly proclaimed by the ringing
of bells, the booming of cannon, and other public
demonstrations. While the Union was exulting over
its first great victory, hundreds of the soldiers who
had been wounded in winning it were taken from the
blood-stained snow, with their garments frozen upon
them.

This was the first battle-field that Mrs. Bickerdyke
saw, and it was one of the most terrible. There were
no available places to be used as hospitals, and many
of the men lay suffering with their clothes unremoved,
and their wounds undressed until they perished. The
country, which was making every effort to relieve
them in their extremity, could not succor them until
hundreds had died. Mrs. Bickerdyke and her small
party witnessed this calamity with courage; and, with
unremitting activity, bent upon relieving as many as
possible. She saw men with mangled limbs lying
upon bare floors, protected only by their soiled and
tattered uniforms, and in the direst want. Perhaps,
as she bent over one with a bowl of broth in her
hand, and a bandage for his wound, the poor sufferer
would say, "I am dying now," and breathing into

her ears a message for those he held most dear, expire
before her eyes. Another less seriously injured,
would be so thankful for her aid that he would express his feelings with tears.

The Confederates who had been hurt were taken
in charge by these willing workers, after having been
deserted by their own surgeons. When ministering
to them it was forgotten that they were fallen foes,
and the kindness they received filled them with
surprise and gratitude, often. touchingly expressed.
"That arm would not have done so well, if I had
known what sort of people I was fighting," said one,
as his shattered arm was being dressed by gentle and
skillful hands.

From a weird incident that occurred here it may
be gathered how courageous and deeply interested
Mrs. Bickerdyke was. Through the darkness that
wrapt the whole landscape at midnight, a strange
light appeared flitting about over the deserted battle-
field, where the dead still lay awaiting burial. This
was seen by an officer who chanced to be looking
out of his tent, and he sent some one to inquire into
the cause of the phantom semblance. He was
startled on the return of his messenger to learn that
it was Mrs. Bickerdyke examining, by the light of a
lantern, those who had been left, because she feared
that some among them might still be alive. She said
that she could not endure the thought that any conscious being was lying out there in the cold and gloom
with the slain. Through that awful field she searched,
not with a grief-stricken heart seeking her kindred,

which might have inspired her with such fearlessness, but only for humanity's sake. Rarely, indeed, does a woman possess such nerve or self-forgetfulness as this.

These harrowing scenes, never to be forgotten by those who passed through them, were, in a measure, ended by the arrival of the hospital steamer, *City of Memphis*, loaded with sanitary stores taken on at Cairo. Physicians arrived from Chicago on the first trains, after telegrams had been sent for them. Two days later a number of sanitary steamers brought efficient relief. Mrs. Bickerdyke accompanied five boat loads of the wounded soldiers, as they were being removed to different hospitals along the rivers. She did all that she could to lessen their pain during these necessary journeys; and succeeded so well that she gained the most sincere confidence and admiration of the officers and surgeons, who could appreciate her remarkable executive ability and endurance. After she had seen the courageous sufferers placed in good care, she turned her attention to another feature of her work, which gained her still greater esteem from those who already recognized her superior abilities. With true feminine caution and forethought, she had the cast-off clothing of the men saved, and succeeded in obtaining an order from the proper authorities to have them cleansed at Savannah. She superintended this task herself, having the washing done by hired contrabands. In view of the battles which were known to be approaching shortly, this was extremely prudent. The army had grown so rapidly that the sanitary projects designed by Government could not at first be of practical benefit when most required; and therefore all resources husbanded for such occasions would be of untold value to those who should need them. Mrs. Bickerdyke realized this. She knew what anguish awaited some of those who would fall wounded at Shiloh, and for their sakes she did not shrink from the hard, self-imposed duty of assorting and having prepared the thousands of soiled articles that would have been utterly worthless but for her; but which, after these exertions, would be applied to many a purple bruise and bleeding hurt, affording ease, and the sweet blessing of purity. Her energy and strength, which had before seemed inexhaustible, gave way while she was engaged in this sickening task, but fortunately the illness lasted only a short time.

Was not her resignation in performing such repulsive work for humanity's sake as noble and self-sacrificing as that of a commander who leads his men into the very jaws of death? It is not the pale-faced nun, cloistered in a lonely cell, who should be pictured as the prototype of self-abnegation; but such a woman as this, strong, high-minded, and capable of overmastering sympathies that cause her to forget every selfish feeling or desire.

In March, Mrs. Bickerdyke went on board the gun-boat, *Fanny Bullet*, and accompanied the 21st Regiment of Indiana Volunteers to Pittsburg Landing. A fleet of more than eighty war steamers moved up the dark waters of the Tennessee in a heavy storm of rain and sleet. Many of them carried troops who had fought at Fort Donelson, and these had walked two miles over the bottom-lands, in ice-cold water, ankle deep, to reach the steamers, where they found crowded apartments and no fires or refreshments. Still they joined in the cheers that went up from the hopeful army. The next morning brought sunshine, and they were welcomed by the songs of birds ringing through the air, and the freshened face of nature smiling around them. Although many of these men had suffered the hardships of war, every one moved with the quick step, and examined his surroundings with the light-hearted curiosity of lads who defied danger. The young leaves were just bursting from their downy sheaths upon trees and saplings, and beneath them blue-bells had begun to open their small cups to the light. Even though the lowlands were damp and unhealthful from the late storms, and the rains that still fell at intervals, this did not lessen the enthusiasm that reigned, and was especially marked among the young volunteers, who were yet filled with the glow of newly awakened patriotism. Many of these soldiers were little more than boys, and among them could be found those who had been cherished as the pride and joy of a whole household.

One like this, Louis R. Belknap, was in the 16th Regiment of Wisconsin Volunteers. He had seen scarcely nineteen years, but was tall and broad shouldered, and had a manly will to master any task that Providence might set before him. Still his cheeks were as blooming, and his dark blue eyes as sparkling as those

of a girl. His father and brothers and sisters loved
him with more fondness than was naturally due from
them, because he had been left in their care a
motherless babe. This blithesome, half-willful boy
was the life of his home, and there he was still called
" little Louis," as he had been when his sunny hair
clustered in ringlets about his neck. The prospects
opening before him were inviting, and he surveyed
them with the confidence which is given by the high
spirits and joy of perfect youth.

Suddenly the clouds of war lowered over the land,
and to him they formed a dark background against
which the gorgeous trappings of the army shone with
dazzling brilliancy. The fancies that had always
been kindled into admiration by heroes were made
real, and appealed to him with the force of action.
Besides, the higher sense of patriotism was awakened.
" What is my life compared to the integrity of this
great land for which so many have already died ? "
was the thought that absorbed all lesser ideas, and
he enlisted at the first call for volunteers, without
having even consulted those who loved him most tenderly. From Camp Grant his letters were full of the
delight he took in a soldier's life. " It is glorious," he
said in one of them; and concluded, " now I am ready
for my first battle, and I hope you are glad to know
that I am willing to die for my country."

At Pittsburg Landing he was in the division under
General Prentiss, which was surprised about sunrise
on the first day. He was one of the brave boys who
rushed to their tents and seized their guns at the

earliest sounds of strife. Nobly he stood performing his duty until he was wounded, and as a comrade was bearing him to the rear a fatal ball struck him. With his expiring breath he said, "Tell my friends that I died on the field of battle." After Shiloh was won, he was buried with the members of his company. He was a generous, noble boy; still, it is better to know that he died bravely as he did, than to be · assured that he is still alive, and had fled like a coward, as so many did that day. So this beautiful youth was placed in a soldier's grave. The precious offering was not in vain, for, years after, General Grant, when describing this battle, wrote of General Prentiss's command, " It had rendered valiant service, and had contributed a good share to the defense of Shiloh."

This triumph, although so costly, was a glory to the land, and thousands of citizens expressed their joy in public demonstrations. Others have pictured, with skill, those mighty contending forces, and shown to whom should be given the laurels of the warrior's wreath. But there is another view, and though it is sad, it invites the attention by the stern beauty of truth, or by its appeal to all that is charitable and tender in the human heart. Who would leave out of the picture of war the prostrate figures of the slain, or forget, in their praise of the victorious heroes, those who had shed their blood in the cause?

While the battle was raging, a brave soldier, who had been disabled in the engagement at Fort Donel-

4

son, lay in his cot listening to the rattle and din of
the fight. This was General C. F. Smith, and Mrs.
Bickerdyke was his attendant, nursing him with the
gentlest care. He awakened in her a high admiration
by his longing to join in the engagement. About
noon of the first day, when the tide of battle seemed
to be against the Federals, he could not be restrained,
but rushed through his tent, exclaiming, " It can't be
—those brave troops will never surrender. They will
fight to the last, and conquer. Oh, that I were with
them ! " He soon joined many of those ranks, but
not to guide them to victory, for they were numbered
with the dead.

Sunday night, after the conflict had ceased until
day should dawn again, the rain poured upon the
cheerless bivouacs; weary soldiers lay on the wet
earth, unprotected from its pitiless streams, and with
sleepless eyes that could not see a single star in the
black heavens, but, instead, the red glare of a shell,
as it sped on its errand of death to the Confederate
encampments. Gun-boats, stationed in the river, sent
these missiles every fifteen minutes during the night.
One soldier said, " I could not sleep, so I spent part of
the dreary hours in carrying water from the creek to
some who were lying in an old house, wounded."
Every available habitation was used to shelter those
who were injured. The surgeons and their assistants
toiled constantly at their humane duties, while their
lamps, glimmering in the darkness, revealed sights
that made the strongest warrior turn away. General
Grant said in regard to one of these scenes, " Some

time after midnight, growing restive under the storm
nd the continuous pain [he had sprained his ankle],
I moved back to the log-house on the bank. This
had been taken as a hospital, and all night wounded
men were being brought in, their wounds dressed, a
leg or an arm amputated, as the case might require,
and everything being done to save life or to alleviate
suffering. *The sight was more unendurable than en-
countering the rebel fire*, and I returned to my tree in
the rain."

Mrs. Bickerdyke did not see this field during the
battle. " I had too much to do for that," she said;
" but as the wounded men were being brought in, although they were suffering severely, their hearts were
so full of the recent occurrences that they could not
help talking about them. As they had been stationed
in different places, and described the scenes from
their various standpoints, I gathered a complete
idea of what had been done. The saddest thing in
my experience was receiving their last messages and
little treasures to be sent home to their families when
death came to relieve them from pain. Such cries
as, ' What will become of my children?' were hardest
of all to bear."

These thrilling words found a full response in the
motherly heart that beat but to soothe and cheer
those who were sacrificing so much for our country's
sake. She worked faithfully, and with remarkable
courage, in a small house that had been placed in her
charge, and where lay seventy wounded soldiers and
eight officers. The rain continued to fall, and before

relief could be obtained by the arrival of hospital
steamers the utmost destitution prevailed, adding extra pangs to those who already suffered as much as
they could endure. Throughout the vast encampment, the tents were filled with sorrowful occupants,
lying upon beds of damp straw. To them the watchful care and gentle touch of such as Mrs. Bickerdyke,
came like ministrations from an angel of mercy. In
these scenes she needed all her strength, and it served
her well; for she found happiness in relieving the
most neglected, besides caring for those who occupied
the house placed in her possession. These men were
fortunate; for with womanly tact, she contrived to
make them feel an influence like that exercised by one
who has in them a personal interest. Indeed, they
could not help becoming sensible of her tender regard, because her sympathies went out to them so
wholly that she never thought of herself, or seemed
conscious that she looked continually upon sufferings,
the sight of which few could endure. Her only
thought during these trying seasons is beautifully expressed in her own simple words: " I kept doing something all the time to make them better, and help them
to get well."

Here, her dress suggested no ideal of grace or fashion, but, instead, was one to which she had scarcely
given a thought. Her movements were not such as
the artist loves to study, still she won more praise and
gave more delight than the fairest belle in her own
high circle. How radiant were her smiles in those
dismal days, as she went and came with a cheering

word and a welcome gift on numberless errands! Doctors and sanitary agents sought her help and counsel, and found them a blessing. Her name was spoken with expressions of gratitude by numberless soldiers, and they remembered it ever after. Toward the last of that terrible week, the encouraging sounds of the long-expected steamers were heard upon the river, and soon they crowded the landing. Up the slippery banks stores for immediate use were taken, and distributed to those who had waited so long for them. As one of the steamers, the *Patten*, had to leave immediately, General Grant permitted her stores to be placed upon his floating head-quarters, the *Tigress*, until a place could be prepared for them; because there was neither building nor tent upon the shore that could serve them for a shelter.

The changeful weather of April gave place to May sunshine, and a large number of the soldiers, who had suffered here so long, were carried back to the pure, invigorating air of the North, and placed in military hospitals there. The governor of Illinois chartered a number of steamboats to bring back the disabled soldiers of that State; and at Chicago the Sanitary Commission undertook the duty of receiving and entertaining veterans who were returning from the scenes of action. This proved to be the nucleus of the celebrated Soldiers' Home at Chicago. Other transports carried the wounded away from Pittsburg Landing to Paducah and to Savannah. Mrs. Bickerdyke went to the latter place, and continued her work there. With an aptitude which springs from originality, she found ways of carrying into effect her ideas, while

another might have waited half baffled for want of
help.   She would not offer to those who possessed the
fastidious appetites of invalids, food from which they
could not help but turn away.   Yet what could be
done to better this state of the diet supply, when all
resources were exhausted?   The whole town was in
want of many necessary things.   This problem remained unsolved until Mrs. Bickerdyke, seemingly
without a second thought, had a large stove placed in
her own room, and there cooked with skill and success the delicate preparations that her patients required.   While she was doing this humane work, sanitary supplies were brought for their relief.   These
timely gifts had been prepared in many a quiet home,
from which they were forwarded to Chicago, and
there received by the Sanitary Commission, re-arranged
and sent in charge of an agent to the places where
they would be of the most service.

"In whose care shall I leave them, and who will
distribute them," the agent inquired of one of the
medical authorities at Savannah.   "With Mrs. Bickerdyke," he quickly answered; "there is not another
here who is more faithful, or would do more good
with them."   One so efficient, and so interested in
caring for the soldiers, could not remain long unrecognized by the Sanitary Commission.   Mrs. Porter; the
wife of an army chaplain, who was connected with
the Commission, was sent from Chicago with a number of nurses to Savannah.   There she met Mrs.
Bickerdyke, and, becoming interested in the same
work, secured their appointments from the Commission, as agents in the military field.

CHAPTER III.

THE long summer days dawned and lingered at Savannah, on the Tennessee River, but the sunlight fell uselessly upon many a neglected field and ravaged orchard. During the afternoons it was shut away from the hospital chambers, for there in the quiet wards were many whose eyes had grown dim from pain and weakness. Mrs. Bickerdyke and Mrs. Porter performed their chosen duties here, as constantly and patiently as two sisters of charity, yet each in her own way. Alike they sacrificed all personal comforts and never thought of recreation or change. Their food was plain, and their dress as simple as possible. They toiled together in harmony that was rendered complete by the difference in their natural attributes. Mrs. Porter had a

compassionate disposition, and was highly cultivated.
Her figure was rather slight and delicate, her com-
plexion pale, and her eyes and hair were dark. The
accents of pity were so often blended with her words
that her voice became permanently low and plaintive;
and her sympathies were expressed so frequently and
so gently, that the soldiers called her the "Angel of
the Hospitals." She was a perfect contrast to Mrs.
Bickerdyke, whose sanguine temperament and independent disposition made her strong and cheerful,
until she seemed to inspire others with hope and
strength, even under the most depressing circumstances.

Above a narrow cot with its snowy counterpane,
Mrs. Porter bent, speaking words of consolation to a
dying boy. Her own countenance was radiant with
deep, pure faith, and her voice, so earnest and tender,
awakened feelings like her own in the listener, filling
his trembling soul with courage and joy. In unnumbered instances like this, she soothed the agonies of
death; and to all who suffered, her ministrations were
a blessing.

Mrs. Bickerdyke made her last round through the
wards at night. The lamps burned low, and many of
the wounded soldiers slept, while others watched with
heavy eyes. Here and there she administered a po-
tion, or some refreshment, as she passed along, caring
for them all. "Are you not tired, Mother Bickerdyke?" inquired one thoughtful fellow, as she served
him.

"What if I am, that is nothing. I am well and

strong, and all I want is to see you so too," she replied in lively tones.

In a few moments afterward, she stood unflinch-
ingly at the surgeon's operating table, and assisted
him while he performed some painful duty. After
this the patient was placed in her charge, and she
gave him all necessary restoratives. " I' shall surely
die now," he murmured, " take a message from me to
my p:or family."

" Now do not talk. You are going to take all your
messages to them yourself; for I know you have a
splendid chance to get well," returned her cheerful
voice.

Long afterward, she said earnestly, " Those men
were very brave, bearing the most terrible sufferings
in a heroic manner, and with little complaint."

July found few soldiers in Savannah. The larger
portion of those who had been taken there with the
shadow of death falling over them, had recovered
health, and departed to rejoin their regiments. Others
less fortunate had returned to their Northern homes,
scarred and disqualified for future military service.

Mrs. Bickerdyke saw with pleasure that the numbers in her charge were rapidly decreasing; still she
did not think of spending a few weeks in rest. Her
step was as firm, and her eye as clear as though she
had not watched with the sick for so many
months. There was work for her to do elsewhere.
At Farmington, the hospital was sadly in want of just .
such services as she was fitted to render. No sooner
was she called to this new and trying scene than she

hastened to gather all sanitary supplies that were not needed at Savannah, and went with them to Farmington. On her arrival there she exclaimed, "Never did a place need cleaning so much as this one does. The men here have scarcely a chance to recover, while they are so uncomfortable."

Immediately she set a number of colored men to work, and in a short time every ward was rendered as fresh and inviting as such places could be.

The progress of the war was southward, along the Tennessee River, and in September a battle was fought at Iuka. Here the Union Army, led by Generals Grant and Rosecrans, bore the national flag to victory; and they marched on amid the cheers and rejoicing that filled the air in consequence of their success. This was a hard fought contest, and several hundred Federal soldiers remained upon the ground wounded. Mrs. Bickerdyke again walked over a blood-stained field, to save from death many a life fast ebbing away for want of immediate succor. Quickly and deftly she stanched the blood flowing from wounds and bound them with skill; in this way saving untold numbers of brave men from the destroyer they had so courageously faced. She accompanied them as they were taken in wagons to the hospital at Farmington, which she had previously arranged for their reception. The numbers here were swelled to nearly fifteen hundred, and made the place uncomfortably full, so it was decided to remove them to the more ample accommodations which could be obtained at Corinth, as soon as the condition of the patients would permit.

At Corinth the academy for the education of young women was converted into a military hospital; and during September it was placed under Mrs. Bickerdyke's charge. This was a beautiful building, situated upon high grounds that sloped downward in every direction, in broad, cultivated lawns.

As the men were being taken in conveyances from Farmington, Mrs. Bickerdyke not only went with them to alleviate sufferings on the painful journey, but did much to prevent the waste that is usual upon such occasions. Owing to limited time and means of transportation, culinary utensils, soiled clothing, and such things as were not absolutely necessary in fitting up the place to which they were going, were frequently left without regard as to what would afterward become of them. With prudent forethought Mrs. Bickerdyke had all these articles packed closely, and when she saw that they were to be left, exclaimed in surprise, "Do you suppose that we are going to throw away those things which the daughters and wives of our soldiers have worked so hard to give us? I will prove that they can be saved, and the clothes can be washed too. Just take them along," she concluded, and her orders were obeyed.

An immense cooking-stove that had been sent to the Farmington hospital, and used there, was left in the woods, as heavy and unnecessary freight. This did not escape Mrs. Bickerdyke, who could appreciate its value, and she had it taken on to Corinth. Here it did good service for many months afterwards. As she became more widely known, her strength of pur-

pose and executive ability gained the confidence and
favor of the authorities, who furnished the means to
carry out her plans, and to extend them indefinitely.
The Academy Hospital was one of the most complete
in the South.   All of its details were Mrs. Bickerdyke's especial care, and beside, she did much other
work, establishing a large diet kitchen and a laundry
that cleaned an abundance of linen for several hospitals in Corinth, besides the one under her own supervision.

The great bales of soiled clothing that she had
saved from being burned were sent in charge of
colored men into the woods, to be washed. This
process lasted nearly a week. After she had made
her round of inspection at the Academy, and given
orders for the day, she mounted a white horse, and
rode away from Corinth, two miles into the forest,
where she found the men kindling fires under the
large iron wash kettles, and handling the clothes with
pitch-forks. They tossed the garments about, reveal-
ing among the folds dark stains of crimson, that filled
the dusky workmen with superstitious dread.   Some
were carrying water from the stream near by, and
others stirring barrels of soft soap with long wooden
ladles, preparing the suds, that foamed and bubbled
over upon the grass.   On the arrival of their mounted
commander, each man felt a thrill of pride to receive
her orders, and execute them in such a way as to win
the word and smile of approval which she never failed
to give, when they were deserved. Neither did she
spare those who merited b lame, and they all knew

that from her they would get their due. Lines were
stretched from tree to tree, and soon the breezes flut-
tered through a thousand pieces of fresh white linen,
that gathered the sweet wood scents and purity from
the sunshine. Like a thrifty housewife, she had the
pieces counted and carefully folded for future use.
The gleam of her white horse often appeared through
the woods, now brilliant with the autumnal glory of
red and golden leaves; and she rode through the
streets watching the troops that came pouring into
Corinth, with discerning eyes. She made all things
ready for the battle that seemed approaching.

After the engagement at Iuka, General Grant had
taken part of the army to Jackson, and the Confederate generals, Van Dorn and Price, perceiving the
division in the Union forces, undertook to recapture
Corinth. General Rosecrans defended this position
with an army twenty thousand strong. On the 3d
of October, 1862, the Federal defenses were attacked,
and a battle ensued, which lasted for two days. With
the first sounds of strife, the ministers of mercy at
the Academy Hospital were prepared to receive the
wounded, and so carefully arranged were the duties
assigned to each that their humane work could be
performed with astonishing dispatch. Their power to
benefit the injured was increased almost twofold
Mrs. Bickerdyke had done her work so thoroughly
that she found more frequent opportunities to follow
the progress of the battle here than at any place
during her previous experience. She said, "From
where I stood I could see the 6th Wisconsin, the

Chicago Light Infantry, and all the big siege guns.
In quick succession flashed from their black mouths
broad sheets of flame and smoke which obscured the
view, while the air seemed to quake with the rolling
peal that followed.   Then the smoke, rising, revealed
the artillerymen preparing with rapid motions another charge.   The infantry were all a mass of lines
and groups, some hurrying, and some standing in
obedience to orders, while the smoke veiled them
here and there; and between the roar of the cannonad-
ing, their ringing cheers and shouts could be heard
with the sharp rattle of musketry."

"The orders to the Board of Trade Regiment, advancing into the hottest of the strife, were, ' Take
aim,' 'Shoot well,' 'Go out double quick.'   As they
obeyed with steadfast courage, a blinding volley of
musketry was poured upon them, and men fell, killed
and wounded, in all directions; then a purple cloud
of smoke hid the startling scene.   Just before engaging in the conflict, these valiant soldiers had marched
twenty-four miles.   They went in twelve hundred
strong, and came out four hundred.   It was their first
engagement, and to most of them, their last; but they
obeyed orders, and fell upon the field to fill soldiers'
graves; and so fulfilled the glorious mission of the
true patriot."

All the afternoon the battle raged fiercer and fiercer.
Constantly recruits were brought up to take the
places of those who had fallen, and the air reverberated with one continuous roar.   Toward evening
when the sun shone red, and with slanting beams,

through the powder smoke, a brigade was hurrying past, and Mrs. Bickerdyke heard that they had been marching with all possible haste since noon. They were covered with dust, and their youthful faces wore a haggard expression from the heat and toil of travel. She knew that they were about to join the conflict, hungry and tired, and was determined that they should have something to eat before going further. The officer in command was asked to allow them to rest for a few moments, but he refused. Still the men heard a strong voice call, "Halt" as they were passing the Academy Hospital. The welcome order thrilled through the ranks, and made the long line stop before any one could consider by whom the command had been given; it would have been almost irresistible under the circumstances if they had known, because nature appealed so strongly in behalf of the measure. With all possible dispatch, each man was given a bowl of soup or coffee. While they were drinking, their canteens were filled with water, and a loaf of bread was supplied to each. Then came the order, "Forward march," and again the brigade was in motion. Their steps were lighter, and their faces were brightened. Only a few minutes had been lost, and these were of no importance in comparison to the added courage and spirit which they immediately manifested in consequence of this much-needed refreshment. For several hours they had been marching, and it was then five o'clock. If they had not stopped, they could have had no food until after midnight, when the tide of war turned in favor of the

Federals. It was Mrs. Bickerdyke who had cried halt, and had given the soldiers food and drink. The story of this heroic act gained favor among them, and from that time after they called her the "General." Her interference in their behalf was more deeply appreciated because many of the men died of hunger, thirst, and fatigue during that hard-fought battle.

In the early part of the first night the Confederate artillery began to shower missiles of destruction almost into the very heart of Corinth. The great shells exploded in the streets, and some fell so near the Academy Hospital that it became necessary for its occupants to move to different quarters. This was a difficult task, and yet, however hazardous it might prove, it had to be done. The surgeons and nurses with their attendants went about the work courageously. Ambulances conveyed the wounded men to a sheltered valley, called Kincaid's Grove. Here a field hospital was arranged, and most of the eighteen hundred men who were brought here found themselves safely and comfortably situated. Few were in any way neglected during the accomplishment of this difficult task, and yet there was something left for the faithful and watchful care of Mrs. Bickerdyke. While the hurried work of pitching the tents and preparing the cots was going on, a young musician, who had been wounded in the morning, was placed with others upon the ground, until more suitable quarter. could be made ready. By some means he was overlooked when the others were taken away. Being too

weak to make himself heard when he called for attention, he must have remained there the rest of the
night if Mrs. Bickerdyke had not made a final round
of inspection with her lantern and discovered him.
"Oh, Mother Bickerdyke!" he exclaimed, in a voice
like that of a frightened child, "I am so glad you
found me, for it is awfully lonesome here."

The morning stars twinkled over this sequestered
valley, where the white tents among the pine and
hemlock trees were secure from danger, although
shells and balls were flying above them. These me-
teor-like missiles fell harmlessly far beyond their retreat. They all remained in Kincaid's Grove until
the battle was ended; but before that time their
numbers had been greatly increased by the addition
of wounded soldiers from the field, and when the
Confederate army beat their retreat, they were obliged
to leave many of their sick and wounded men to the
benevolent care of the victorious Federals.

Soon the Academy Hospital re·eived again those
who had been taken out of it that perilous night,
and besides, others who claimed its shelter, until every
cot was full. Large numbers still remained unpro-
vided for, and these were placed in tents pitched
upon the broad lawns about the building. Here and
there, all over the slopes which were now withering
from neglect, could be seen the furrows that had been
plowed by balls and shells, as they sped on their
courses of destruction. Surgeons and nurses found
their duties increased until it was impossible to add
anything more. Every hour of the day and night

5

found tireless feet hurrying upon kindly errands, and
yet there prevailed the discomfort due to insufficient
help and room.   In the tents upon the lawns the patients were cared for by men employed as nurses, and
besides their necessary ministrations, which were performed hurriedly, no other attention was paid to
them except the visits from the doctors.

A young soldier, William Spinning, who belonged
to the 1st Kansas Cavalry, was placed in a tent
with nearly one hundred others who were sick with
fever.   He had always known the comforts of a home,
and the loving care of a mother, in the sickness or
trials which heretofore had fallen to his lot.   Besides,
he was of a refined and studious disposition, which
made his sufferings under the present circumstances
more difficult to endure.   For weeks he lay upon his
narrow cot, languishing in pain, and strove to maintain the courage of a true soldier.   He was young
and ambitious, and the spirit of youth, which touches
with prismatic colors all future prospects, kept him
hopeful until his form was wasted, and his strength
was almost gone.   The step of the attendant sounded
heavily upon the beaten earth that, alone, composed
the floor of the tent, as he came through the entrance at one end.   He paused to pour castor oil
from a large bottle into an iron spoon, and then
gave it to the occupant of the nearest cot.   Proceed-
ing to the second, he gave him a similar dose, and
so on until he reached the last one in the row, after
which he returned along the opposite side.   How
sickening it was to swallow the distasteful medicine

from such a spoon, and after so many fever-parched lips had touched it! Is it any wonder that so many of the men died there? The poor fellow to the right, so near William Spinning's cot that he had often reached over the intervening space to help arrange the coverlids, 'expired one night; and before dawn the bed had been prepared for another, who was placed in it. These trying scenes at last made the young cavalryman succumb to despondency, and to lose all desire to live. When the man at his left hand died, he thought, "I will be the next one taken out, as wasted and ghastly as he is now." He refused to swallow the sickening dose of oil when it was offered, but the attendant forced it down his throat, and went on.

One morning he heard a woman's voice, a ringing, cheerful voice it was, and the sound so unfamiliar aroused his attention. Turning feebly in his cot he saw the figure of a woman standing in the door of the tent, against the background of sunlight. Soon she came in, making inquiries of the attendant as to the condition of the patients under his charge, and also asking them, as she passed along, how they were, and what was given to them. Every face wore a brightened expression as she proceeded, and she took such a motherly interest in them that each one seemed to feel as though some dear friend or relative was visiting him. William Spinning had been anxious to see her when she first entered, and this slight excitement heightened his fever spell so that when she reached him his thin cheek, mantled with a hectic flush, was glowing like red coral, and his large, dark eyes glistened with a feverish light. His hair was matted and damp, and the veins in his temples throbbed visibly. Mrs. Bickerdyke understood his condition at a glance, and, clasping his hot hand, exclaimed, " My poor boy, I am going to do something for you myself."

"Hand me the bay rum," she demanded of a nurse, and, seating herself upon the cot, she took his head in her lap and bathed it tenderly with the fragrant spirits from the decanter. While she was doing this, she talked to him in low, cheerful tones about his future prospects, and told him that it was his duty to live, if only for the sake of those who cared so much for him at home. " They long to see you back again, well and strong. Indeed, you know just how glad they would be to welcome you; so, my brave lad, pluck up courage and get out of this dull tent into the field again. The old flag needs you, and we all need the aid of your strong arms," she concluded, still smoothing his brow with her cool hands. Tears shone in his eyes while he listened; and his whole frame seemed infused with new life and hope as she made him realize that he had a work to do which would be prized by both his kindred and his country. In this way she re-awakened his desire to live, and revived the ambition that had smoldered almost into ashes. Before she left him his face wore a changed expression, and his fever was much subdued. He expressed his gratitude in touching words, and besides, as she went away from the tent, she was followed by blessings from every sufferer there.

For a long time William Spinning lay still, conscious only of soothing words and hopeful thoughts, until the blessed repose of natural and healthful sleep banished, for a time, all consciousness. Long before, he had heard of Mother Bickerdyke, as the soldiers were apt to call her. Then he was vigorous and full of spirits, and his thoughts dwelt upon his uniform and lively horse, and upon the active duties which lay before him, although the crippled soldier who came to the camp-fire with stories of her courage and motherly care, found in him an interested and sympathetic listener. After experiencing the bitterness of pain, and the wonderful power to soothe and cheer, which Mrs. Bickerdyke possessed, he often said, gratefully, " She saved my life, and she has saved numberless others when they were just as wretched and hopeless as I was then."

Her name became popular for miles around every place that had been blessed with her presence; and, mounted upon her white horse, she passed almost anywhere within the Federal lines unquestioned; for to every one her figure and the nature of her errands were familiar. The last time that William Spinning saw her during the war, was under memorable circumstances. He was recovering slowly from his fever when the hospital was moved from Corinth, and in the disturbance of this occasion he, among others, chanced to be left for a short time in the woods. Before the arrival of conveyances to take them away, Mrs. Bickerdyke came to them with refreshments and medicine. She found the young man whom she had helped so graciously in the tent, lying beneath a tree, weak and languid. The autumn air was sharp, and the ground was covered with damp pine needles that served him for a bed. "She treated me as she did the others," said he, "but she was so kind to us all that I never forgot the circumstance."

In a few moments she had rendered every one there more comfortable and cheerful. Probably they all remember her as gratefully as Mr. Spinning does, and at the mention of her name, recall her pleasant voice and motherly care, which proved as refreshing as they were unexpected in those lonely woods. She always went like some beneficent spirit into the most dismal and sequestered nooks. Her noble nature could not brook neglect of the obscure and helpless. Such as these aroused all of her strongest feelings, and she sought them out constantly, as the objects of her special attention. An appeal from the weak or young was perfectly irresistible to her. Because the officers received more pay than the privates, and usually were better able to help themselves in times of sickness, she devoted herself more particularly to the common soldiers. Not the least distinction did she ever make between them, on account of their positions in the army, when they were under her charge. She guarded like a sentinel the sanitary stores, and was implacable in her resentment, if she found any of them misappropriated. When instances of this kind were discovered, she dealt very summarily with the offenders, and made such an example of them that their selfishness was seldom imitated. Incidents of this sort never took her from her post of duty. Usually she reported such miscreants directly to headquarters. She had no fear of their enmity, and no matter how powerful such persons might be, she never overlooked anything from motives of policy.

For more than a year and a half Mrs. Bickerdyke had followed in the footsteps of war along the Mississippi and up the Tennessee Rivers, doing work as useful as any performed by the men who carried muskets, before she thought of taking any rest or change. Although she was so full of endurance and self-reliance, her influence was in every way that of a true, noble woman, and carried something of the atmosphere of home into the hospital and field. Not for a day in all that time had she relaxed her efforts to do thoroughly every duty that lay in her path; and by reason of her superb strength, both physical and mental, she had succeeded wonderfully well. The simple, childish letters that had come from her little boys, at intervals, were to her a source of pleasure and pride. Now she concluded to take a trip back to Galesburg for the purpose of seeing them, and of obtaining a much-needed rest and change. Besides, she desired to know that they were advantageously situated. After all those trying and exciting scenes through which she had so recently passed, it was a delicious sensation to be at home once more, and with the children that she so fondly loved. The well-known streets, and the dear, familiar faces were welcomed again with feelings which must have been like those of a soldier on his return home, after having

escaped the perils of disease and warfare. By the
bright, crackling blaze in the fire-place, she told to interested listeners the tales of army life, that are so
thrilling when they are gleaned from experience.
The snow-flakes whirled gleefully about the eaves, as
if wild with delight. They made the summer and
autumn retreat farther and farther southward, until the
whole plains were white with their uniforms. Receiving people who came to make inquiries about
their absent dear ones, was here one of Mrs. Bickerdyke's daily occupations. In her active life, she had
met not a few of them, and whether her news was
such as to give pleasure or pain, she was always kind
and sympathetic. She had to deliver many of those
messages and tokens, sent by soldiers, who had died,
to their friends. Such remembrances always cause
heartaches, even if they are a melancholy solace to
those who receive them. Protected by thick wraps,
Mrs. Bickerdyke made her way over the snowy walks
to many a dwelling, where she knew her errand would
make tears flow; yet even from such duties as these
she never shrank, but went to those who were mourning at the hearth-side as readily as to the field. Here,
too, her courage and tenderness were just as welcome.
She said that she was always lucky in finding these
places. It is not remarkable that she seemed fortunate in this respect, because she held such missions
sacred, and bent all of her powerful energies to fulfill
them to her own satisfaction. She would clasp her
arms about some sobbing woman, and, holding before
her tearful eyes the little picture, or other token, tell

her how her soldier boy, or husband, or lover died bravely and willingly for the glorious old flag. Recalling their parting, when feelings of patriotism rose high, she repeated the last words with which she was intrusted, and which always glowed with love for the dear ones at home and for the land.

Besides, she was self-commissioned with pleasanter work, which was also more suited to her lively disposition. She had been to the front, and knew what gifts were of the most benefit to the brave men there. Committees from aid societies, and wives and daughters of the soldiers came flocking to her for the purpose of learning what she could tell so well concerning these things Her resolve was to do all that she could to encourage and stimulate them to exertions which she knew were truly charitable as well as patriotic. In this her usual good fortune attended her, and Galesburg was enlivened by many successful sociables and fairs held for the purpose of collecting money and all kinds of useful articles to be sent to the Sanitary Commission at Chicago.

Advantage was taken of the holidays, which are always observed with festivities, to secure gifts for the soldiers. This proved no difficult task, as so many families missed from their circles a member who had joined the volunteers, and thoughts of the war were constantly with them. Patriotic expressions appeared in every feature of social life and religious worship. Even the children awoke Christmas morning to find gifts of toy drums and swords, or whole regiments of wooden soldiers. The clatter of their mimic arms blended with the pealing of bells that proclaimed as usual from the church towers, " Peace on earth and good-will toward men."

The parlors of the quaint little church, which Mrs. Bickerdyke attended in Galesburg, were the scene of many entertainments given to benefit the soldiers.

See yonder a bevy of girls filling a box with all sorts of useful things for them. One of the merriest contributes a bundle of socks, with an audacious little note pinned into a toe of each pair. Another, scarcely more serious, excuses the needle-work upon a couple of shirts which she has made, by saying that she can make better bread than button-holes, and asking the soldier who may chance to wear the shirts to come and see for himself, when the war is over, if he is not so fortunate as to have a wife. They chatter among themselves, as girls always do when together, and little speeches, half witty or comical, and half in earnest, flow uninterrupted by their occupation.

" We put up a lot of chickens to send," remarked one, " but Mother Bickerdyke says they are better kept at home, because such things are likely to spoil on the way." " But here are a lot of dried plums to make sauce of, and a pair of slippers." Perhaps upon something packed away by this merry group, tears had fallen from the loveliest eyes, as it was being finished at some lonely evening hour. What heart-aches many of them endured, because of the absent ones who were so fondly loved.

It was Mrs. Bickerdyke's privilege to distribute the contents of countless boxes sent by such girls as

these to the Sanitary Commission, and from thence to
the hospitals. She witnessed occurrences of the
most pathetic nature, as well as scenes of merriment,
and romantic incidents occasioned by their random
gifts and missives.

Midwinter reigned over the whitened earth, and the
air was sharp with cold. Those dauntless little conquerors, the snow-flakes, gained supremacy over the
weather, but they had no power to stay the march of
war. During all of these inclement months the
soldiers never relaxed the struggle for victory. The
holidays had not found the larger portion of the
Union forces snugly settled in winter quarters, and
enjoying impromptu feasts around the roaring camp-
fires, as they had last year. Then, when not on duty,
their time had been spent in pleasant occupations.
To them the huts and tents had quite a homelike air,
after they had been occupied for a few weeks. About
the walls upon pegs hung their muskets and other
equipments, and empty boxes and barrels as well as
roughly hewn logs, formed their furniture. Some
spent the days and long evenings carving in wood,
while others played cards or chess. The musicians,
too, contributed a good share to their simple enjoy-
ments, and many a lively tune and merry song cheered
the winter days.

But now, instead of all these comforts and amusements, they were ordered upon long marches over
muddy roads, and through marshy swamps. Often
the rain poured upon them all day, and at night they
slept in their wet garments, sheltered only by tents

pitched upon the storm-beaten earth. The exposure, and scanty rations meted out to them, made sickness and death their constant companions. News of these sufferings reached their friends and kindred in the North, and filled them with gloom. Owing to the storms and the rapid movements of the several commands, it was very difficult to effect communication between them and those who were anxious to give them aid. Nurses and surgeons went South constantly to the hospitals, and many anxious wives and mothers would have been glad to go if it had been possible. Home, which is the most delightful of all places the earth contains, is rendered incomparably dismal when bereft of those who give to it the charm that makes it seem enchanted.

Countless numbers of the soldiers broke this spell of happiness when they went to the war; and now that they needed the love and care which they had left, every patriotic heart yearned to supply their wants. Mrs. Bickerdyke, with her rich experience and fine capabilities, hastened to those scenes where she could be of such benefit to her people and her country.

CHAPTER IV.

DURING the war Memphis was selected as a center for military headquarters and hospitals. The grand Mississippi, that wound along its outskirts, afforded a direct highway northward, where the people were anxious to aid and encourage the army by all means in their power; and from Memphis it flowed into the very battle-fields. Steamers came puffing down upon its turbid waters, loaded with recruits, and all manner of stores; and they bore up from the South thousands of sick and wounded soldiers, who had become disabled amid the scenes of suffering and carnage at the front of war. Tents clustered about the suburbs of the town among man-

(77)

sions from which the owners had sent their families
into distant cities, and joined either the Federal or
Confederate forces.   Men in uniform were seen upon
the emerald lawns, instead of merry children and fair
women.   No sounds came echoing among the lofty
trees from the school bells and church bells, for the
teachers of science and religion had gone to labor in
less peaceful scenes.   In the city, stores and ware-
houses were no longer filled with the noise and hum
of business; but instead, the haunts of traffic were
appropriated for barracks and hospitals, and daily
the streets were filled with the sounds of marching
feet and martial music.

Mrs. Bickerdyke arrived here early in January,
1863.   The incessant storms gave everything a chill
and drenched appearance, while the work for such as
she was overwhelming both in amount and in its
nature; and yet the dismal skies and heavy tasks had
no power to affect her courage and sunny disposition·
She began the first work that was offered to her with
resolution.   This was the preparation of the Adams'
Block Hospital, which occupied a whole square of
new brick buildings designed for stores.   In this her
assistance was of much value.   Nine hundred cots
were placed in rows about the lofty chambers, and
made comfortable, as well as pleasing in appearance,
by their snow-white pillows and counterpanes.   These
were for the soldiers wounded in the recent battles,
and who were expected as soon as they could be
moved from the field hospitals and barges where they
had been placed immediately after being hurt.   Ac-

commodations were arranged for six thousand men; and besides, there were a number of hospitals already established in Memphis. The medical director and the medical inspector authorized Mrs. Bickerdyke to visit many of the latter and improve them, as they were not in as good a condition as they should have been. Her influence in these places was shown particularly by their extra cleanliness in all respects. Immense supplies of linen were needed for the disabled soldiers, and she went energetically to work, establishing a laundry large enough to meet the demand. She did this, besides attending faithfully to the duties which she had previously assumed. The wholesome effect of fresh linen she estimated at its full value. By means of her own exertions and influence, she made it possible for every hospital in Memphis to enjoy an unlimited supply of clean clothing and bedding, which were as important as care and medicine, to promote comfort and the return of health.

Day after day, Mrs. Bickerdyke was occupied with these humane pursuits, going and coming always with a firm step and cheerful face. The storms of that remarkable winter kept the heavens overcast with rain clouds, and swelled the volume of the great Mississippi far beyond its banks. The Union forces, unwilling to relinquish an inch of the territory that they had so dearly won, steadfastly held their ground, or kept pushing southward amid dismal swamps and marshes, where the air was humid with malaria; and hunger and cold pursued them like wolves. With

valiant hearts they pressed on, having but a single
goal in view, and that the crown of victory. Their
patriotism scorned the fury of the tempest and the
power of even the most insufferable privations, as
well as the Confederate shot and shell. These hardships were endured with such fortitude as to prove
every soldier a hero. The tattered uniform and the
wasted cheek may call for pity, but the ringing voice
and kindling glance reveal the will and valor that rise
supreme above every trial of war, and compel the
homage due to the conqueror.

Though their physical strength gave way under
these circumstances, their spirits were unsubdued.
Men constantly fell in the ranks from exhaustion,
and these were taken northward to Memphis as soon
as possible. The shrill scream of the hospital fleet
whistles announced their arrival every day. Mrs.
Bickerdyke cared for these with more than her usual
tenderness, because she realized how they had hun-
gered for a word of sympathy and interest, as well as
for the necessaries of life. Her manner of express-
ing the deep feelings which she entertained for them
was most admirable. It was not natural for her to
bend over a sufferer's cot with dewy lashes, and
breathe, in cooing tones, expressions of sorrow for
his pain, and admiration for his fortitude. Her practical disposition made her appreciate more keenly the
necessities of the present and future, than the trials of
the past. Cheerful smiles and encouraging words
made her presence always welcome. Besides, she
never came but for a purpose, her hands being ever

full of gifts or busy at some task. When she had extra or special stores to distribute, her devotion to the soldiers made her joy almost equal to their own, and she gave them in a most noble and unselfish way.

"Here is something that the folks at home have sent to you," she would say. Then her pleasant voice would ring out assuringly, "You need never fear that they are forgetting the boys who follow the flag." With sentences like these she soon obtained the whole story of the soldier's home-life, in the telling of which he forgot his own trials, and accepted the garment or food which she had brought, feeling as though it had come from the loving hands of his own wife or mother. Whatever was in her power to bestow was given so heartily and cheerfully that it always possessed a greater value in the eyes of its recipient than it would have otherwise. It was true maternal sympathy for the soldiers that made her capable of touching each one's heart in this remarkable way, and made many a manly voice call her "mother," in tones as gentle as though he had really addressed his own mother.

Upon the magnolias, great buds began to swell and burst their waxen calyxes with rich hues of rose color, and the southern pines and cedars flaunted new fringes of pale green upon their somber robes. Earth was awakening again to the life and beauty of springtime. Sunlight touched with edges of gold the outlines of every spray and flower, and the birds twittered to each other the secrets of their hidden nests and the pearl-like treasures within them. Nature

6

seemed trying to make amends for the severity of
the winter, by lavishing everywhere her rarest charms.

While sunbeams came through the open window
with dancing zephyrs, perfumed from the verdant
hills, it seemed difficult to realize that they lingered
upon men racked with disease and burning with feverish pain; that Death, with his hollow eyes and
emaciated figure, was personified by tortured and
helpless beings to whom there came no ministering
hand. Yet Doctor Irvin, the medical director at
Memphis, went to Mrs. Bickerdyke one morning to
consult with her about such a scene as this. It was
the small-pox hospital, called Fort Pickering, which
had relapsed into so dreadful a condition that no
help could be obtained for the purpose of renovating
it. "Nine men lie within its walls awaiting burial,
and more are dying," he concluded.

When Mrs. Bickerdyke volunteered to go herself,
the doctor was startled by her intrepidity. He ob-
jected, also, because of her great usefulness where she
then was, and said that she could not be spared from
her present duties. However, her noble soul was en-
lidest in the cause of their release from so terrible a
situation, and she could not be dissuaded from her
purpose. What unprecedented courage must have
been exercised to make a woman willing to undertake so revolting a task! The place was the abode
of an infectious disease that had almost turned it
into a charnel-house, and the very air within its walls
was poison. Her heroic conduct on this occasion
proved her to be perfectly fearless, and oblivious to

those natural desires which make personal ease and luxury so ardently sought. She realized only that her country's sons were dying for want of care, and she turned to them with the unfailing devotion of a true mother, that has scarcely a parallel. Indeed, the strength and wisdom which her success here proved her to possess beyond question, excite scarcely less admiration than her unbounded charity.

All ordinary methods of cleansing and renovating a hospital were in vain here. The place had to be reorganized in almost every respect. The taint and venom of all foulness that had found a lodgment in those dingy wards, where sounded the groans of pain and despair, fled before her presence as the vampire takes flight at the approach of dawn. Within a few days after she entered, this place could scarcely be recognized as the one put under her charge. A clean and airy appearance soon distinguished all of the apartments. In them suitable and appetizing food was served, while method and order were apparent in every detail of the arrangements and work of the entire place. The blessings of temporal comforts, and woman's gentle services, were to those sufferers what food is to the famishing. Mrs. Bickerdyke's willing hands brought to them the elixir of life, and to each one the precious nectar was given without stint or measure.

Heaven spared the soldiers' mother, and she came from those shunned hospital doors, strong and uncontaminated by the dreadful contagion which she had banished. No scars marred her benign counte-

nance, to remind those who looked upon it of her
faithful love and dauntless courage. After having
endured the hardships and shared the exile of those
forsaken sufferers, she was wholly free again to enjoy
the pursuit of her benevolent work. As she resumed
her former active occupations, how pleasant must
have appeared the quiet mansions surrounded by
their green lawns, the bright flower plots, above which
bloomed the queenly magnolias, and even the restless throngs of life that poured in and out of the city.

Her hazardous task being accomplished, she immediately assumed the position of matron in the Gayoso
Block Hospital. About six hundred men, who had
been wounded at Arkansas Post, were placed in the
wards here; and they were fortunate, because Mrs.
Bickerdyke made this the most home-like and
comfortable place that they could have occupied in
Memphis. It also had the advantage of being furnished with all of the appliances which should be
found in such an institution. A short season of
peace and order characterized the time which was
spent here. Though men arrived each day to fill the
vacant cots, until over one thousand had assembled
under the roof of this hospital, everything was done
in the most approved way, and many a patient acknowledged his appreciation of his good fortune by
saying that even in his own home he would not have
been cared for more tenderly or efficiently.

This orderly and well-kept place was no more bar-
ren of incidents than were the field hospitals. Sometimes a woman made her appearance inquiring for

her wounded son or husband, and she generally remained until the soldier whom she came to benefit
could be sent home with her. These women always
remembered Mrs. Bickerdyke with grateful hearts,
and pressed upon her invitations to visit their homes,
besides showing other marks of gratitude. A mother
kneeling by the cot of her son, who was scarcely
more than a boy, being only seventeen years old, said,
with tears in her eyes, "It is no wonder that you are
called mother here, for you treat these men every
one with so much kindness and patience. I owe to
you the preservation of my darling's life. Oh! it
would have broken my heart if I had found him
dead." With the thought she burst into a passion of
sobs, and buried her face in the white pillow, upon
which her son's head lay. He smoothed her silver
hair gently with his one hand, for he had lost the
other, and consoled her with words of filial affection·

Scenes of this kind were frequent, and yet they
always filled Mrs. Bickerdyke with feelings for which
she could find no expression.

Her services were devoted especially to the private
soldiers. Officers who chanced to need them, were
never distinguished by extra attentions on account of
their positions. She quaintly describes her own conduct in this respect, by remarking, "I always treated
an officer as well as a private, and if he put on airs,
it did not make any difference either. He was served
in turn with the others, just like any soldier." She
sometimes met with opposition from the officers whose
duties were connected with the hospitals. The prin-

cipal reasons for this were, her dislike of the formality
and restraint which they often considered necessary
to military discipline, and her habit of criticising their
actions, if they did not reach the standard of her approval. To all who were in any way dishonest, or
incompetent to fill their positions, she was the neme-
sis who pursued them relentlessly. Her object was
to benefit the soldiers, and she would not countenance
for a moment anything to their disadvantage. Frequently those who disliked her at first, being preju-
diced by her independent and confident bearing, became, on further acquaintance, her most sincere
friends, appreciating keenly her efficiency and importance in the work that was of mutual interest.

Col. W. W. Jackson, of General Hurlburt's staff,
relates an incident that illustrates the confidence that
was placed in her judgment by those in authority.
Several hundred negroes were employed to labor in
the hospitals. These were runaway slaves from the
southern plantations, who had gathered at Memphis
in large numbers. For the most part they were poor
creatures, half-clad and half-starved, having been several weeks in the swamps and waste lands, while elud-
ing their pursuers. Some were bright, well-trained
fellows, possessing enough energy to make themselves
useful to the people to whom they had fled for pro-
tection; and many of them rendered valuable services
in the hospitals and laundries. One of the surgeons
of the regular army, ordered all of these colored em-
ployés to be discharged; at the same time directing
that their duties should be performed by convalescents.

This course provoked a remonstrance from Mrs. Bickerdyke, whose sympathies were thoroughly interested in behalf of the soldiers. She could not endure to see those who had just risen from beds of suffering, many of them having narrowly escaped death, engaged in work that required not only much physical strength, but also nervous force and endurance. These men were emaciated, and weak from pain. Many of them were so anxious to rejoin their regiments that everything which delayed the return of health was doubly hard to bear, since the enthusiastic spirit, as well as the enfeebled frame, was tortured. When Mrs. Bickerdyke heard that men like these were ordered to perform such hard and wearing labor, a host of their pale faces rose before her imagination, impelling her to do something to prevent such a calamity from falling upon them; and her generous impulse brooked no delay.

This occurred late in the evening. The rain was pouring outside and the streets were covered with mud, and only half illuminated by the flickering lights that seemed to be blinking through their spattered and dripping glasses. Mrs. Bickerdyke looked out upon this forbidding scene, yet it did not cause her to hesitate.

She ordered a conveyance, and was soon at headquarters, where General Hurlburt, who was in command at Memphis, received her cordially, and gave her a written authorization to retain the services of the negroes, who were employed in the hospitals; and directing the surgeons to do all in their power to carry out her wishes.

Those officers, who were notably considerate of their men, awakened enthusiastic admiration in Mrs. Bickerdyke. "They were grand," she once exclaimed. "Usually they shared all the privations of the soldiers, and I have seen them as hungry and dusty and tired as any private in the ranks. One evening I offered a colonel a delicious cup of tea, when he was almost overcome with fatigue. He waved it away and, pointing to a cot near by, said 'Give it to the lad. He needs it more.' The young man designated had been suffering for a long time, and his extreme thinness and pallor must have attracted the colonel's notice."

The higher officers, who had an opportunity to observe her work and become acquainted with her, always appreciated thoroughly the great services she rendered the army. Generals Grant, Sherman, and Logan were impressed with her admirable character, and showed their confidence by allowing great latitude in the pursuit of her labors for the soldiers.

While the military movements in the vicinity of Vicksburg were taking place, men arrived constantly at Memphis from those scenes, disabled from exposure and hardships, or from wounds received in the various engagements with the Confederates. The rivers and bayous were swollen so much that the swamp lands, through which the soldiers marched, were often submerged to a depth of several feet. The Federals suffered many hardships in their attempts to reach a point from which Vicksburg could be attacked advantageously. Even General Sherman led his men on foot through dense cane brakes in the darkness of night, with only the flickering rays of candles to guide them.

The commodious hospitals in Memphis had not been prepared in vain, for about eleven thousand sol-diers were provided for within them. Mrs. Bicker-dyke visited the different institutions frequently, be-sides performing her duties as matron of the Gayoso Hospital. Her experience as a housewife had made her familiar with the principles of economy, and here she was always planning to give the patients more and better food and care with the means at hand, than were already provided. Fresh milk and eggs were supplied in scant quantities, and were poor in quality. Besides, the prices were extremely high. She declared that it was perfect nonsense to give forty cents a quart for milk that resembled chalk and water. This was a source of annoyance common to all, and she determined to find a remedy for the evil, as such food was very important in the diet of the sick. The project formed in her active mind was considered impracticable—even visionary at first; but her judg-ment was not at fault, and her forcible arguments soon overcame all opposition. Sanction to carry out her plans was gained from the proper authorities, and so, just as spring was merging into summer, she started North upon her famous "cow and hen mis-sion." Her object was to obtain one hundred cows and one thousand hens to supply the hospitals with an abundance of fresh milk and eggs at a small cost. They were to be cared for by freedmen upon an island in the Mississippi, near Memphis. The generous character of the Northwestern farmers she knew well, and could safely rely upon them for assistance. Even the first stage of this mission was distinguished. More than one hundred crippled soldiers accompanied her as far as St. Louis. There was not one of these poor, maimed fellows who did not leave her with a blessing, when she saw them safely into a hospital of that city. While she was standing among them, they made a striking group—one that might serve as a model for Liberty caring for the sons who had suffered in her cause.

As soon as Mrs. Bickerdyke made her plan known in Jacksonville, Illinois, one of the wealthy farmers there, Mr. Strawn, aided by a few of his neighbors, gave her the hundred cows she desired; and as she proceeded further, chickens seemed to spring up in her path. Her arrival at Milwaukee was heralded by the lowing of cows, and the cackling of hens; and when she reached Springfield the same welcome sounds greeted her. This was one of the most peculiar of her varied experiences. It savors of the fantastic stories told in fairy books. Little girls with dimpled cheeks and shy, bright eyes, came to her with plump hens, scolding and clucking in their arms; and old women brought like treasures in their baskets. Then a farmer would come leading by the horns a cow and say that for the sake of a son or a brother "down there a fighting the gray coats," he would send her along too. Her sleek sides were softly patted in a sort of farewell, while she instinctively lowed to a little calf in some neighboring barn.

Mrs. Bickerdyke visited Chicago, where she was entertained by Mrs. Livermore, another lady celebrated for her earnest labors in behalf of the soldiers during the war. It was a Sabbath afternoon, and the sun hung low when the guest arrived and was welcomed to her quiet home. Here the family were preparing to attend the marriage of some neighboring friends, and, although Mrs. Bickerdyke had taken no rest since her arrival in the city, she preferred to join them rather than to retire. The clear bells that pealed in the twilight from numerous church towers, served as the wedding bells; and the ceremony was a quiet one performed in the bride's own home. To the surprise of Mrs. Bickerdyke, a young officer in his handsome uniform took the bridegroom's place beside the white-robed girl, and after he had introduced her as his wife to Mrs. Bickerdyke, he surprised her still more by saying that they had previously met at Fort Donelson. Then he reminded her of an officer there, who had been wounded by a minié-ball, appealing in vain to a surgeon to save his leg, until she interfered in his behalf. She persuaded the surgeon to leave him until the next day, when it was found that he could recover without undergoing the painful loss. "I never can express my gratitude," he concluded, "for you saved me from being so terribly maimed, and I do indeed feel that you have been to me a second mother."

While upon this tour, her pleasing appearance and cordial manners, and the unique character of her mission, impressed the people whom she visited agree-

ably. They made many attempts to show her public
attentions, but she modestly shrank from such demonstrations of personal favor. Still she gained the
good-will of all when she expressed with the force
and simplicity of truth her appreciation of their
kindness to her and to those whom she sought to aid.

The heat of early summer was ripening the corn
on the outlying plantations about Memphis, and
making the roads deep with dust, as she again returned to her duties there. Below, along the banks
of the Mississippi, this hot, unhealthful season had
no power to impede the progress of war; and the
roar of artillery sometimes seemed to mock the
crashing peals of the thunder-storms. All the rivers
and bayous were low, and the swamps exhaled the
rank and poisonous odors of the rich semi-tropical
vegetation half sweltered in the heat. The army
was engaged in the long, exciting siege of Vicksburg
that kept the spirits of the soldiers high with hope,
and encouraged them to make every effort in their
power to achieve the object of the campaign. Such
exertions in the blazing heat of the Southern climate,
made large numbers sick with fever. The assaults
upon the impregnable stronghold, that took place in
June, caused many of the brave fellows, who toiled
up the bluffs of Vicksburg, to fall bleeding upon the
parched earth.

New clusters of white tents sprang up among the
groves in the vicinity. They were for the sick and
wounded men, who were forced by their inability to
be moved, to lie in these frail shelters, and listen to

the screaming of shells and the sharp rattle of musketry, that sounded from the direction of the belea-
guered city; and nearer, the rumble of teams and the
hoarse shouts of the drivers were heard at intervals·
A moment of silence was intensified by the murmur
of the green and balsam-scented pines, which only
half shut out the burning sunbeams. Mrs. Bickerdyke was needed here much more than in Memphis,
and she was soon among the sufferers, bringing welcome supplies and comfort with her. Lemons and
ice she mixed into draughts, which tasted like nectar
to the lips of thirsty men who lay prostrated by fever.
They had been longing for pure water, in the place
of which, that dipped from the warm and murky currents of the river was offered to them.

Often in the sultry summer nights, when the stars
twinkled feebly through the humid atmosphere, Mrs.
Bickerdyke went from tent to tent, with a great, brown
pitcher of cold and sparkling lemonade, refreshing
each soldier with an overflowing cupful. Now and
then a lizard or a serpent would glide across her path,
and owls hooted from the dense pines and cypress
trees in the darkness beyond; but to these she never
gave a thought. Perhaps she noticed the shells that
frequently described their fiery flight across the dark
skies, sent from the Union mortars over the defenses
of Vicksburg; still the feeble rays of the candles in
the tents interested her more. They were the beacons
to guide her to her posts of duty. Insects flew hum-
ming through the shadows, to scorch their glittering
wings in those red lights, while others more vicious

circled above the cots seeking their prey. Mrs. Bickerdyke's willing hands found little rest. Her tender
heart was wrung by the pitiful appeals of the dying,
calling upon her in the delirium of fever for their absent friends; or giving in high, excited voices the
cheers of victory, or the groans of the wounded.
Yet her strong nerves were proof against even long-
continued scenes like these. She awoke early in the
golden summer dawns, and brushed the dew from her
path as she began the labors of another day. With
clear eyes she looked upon her duties, and her voice
was strong and cheerful when she spoke to the suffering men, who always welcomed her so gladly. Hope
and comfort took possession of every tent she entered,
and amid these trying circumstances she was the
same energetic and practical woman, whom the soldiers had honored with the title of "General," at Corinth. Here, also, she displayed the same interest in
every one that had made her so popular there. One
day she rode from the river in an ambulance loaded
with sanitary stores for the hospital. After everything had been taken out of the vehicle, the driver
was about to start away, when she said, "Wait a moment, Mr. Lillibridge, I have something for you."

The young soldier was pleased at hearing himself so
pleasantly addressed, and thought that she must be a
witch to divine his name. He was almost convinced,
when she handed him a large package which proved
to be composed of fresh and rare eatables, that served
as an uncommon treat to him and half a dozen comrades. The meal was an agreeable surprise, long re-

membered by them all. Mrs. Bickerdyke seemed to know every one's name instinctively, and whoever she spoke to felt that she was particularly interested in himself. It is not surprising that she won such universal respect and esteem from those men. They often came to her with their little treasures, if they anticipated exposure to any imminent peril; and they placed hundreds of dollars of their pay in her hands for safe keeping. She was indeed trusted and honored as much as though the word " mother," by which they all called her, was something more than a mere figurative appellation.

Vicksburg surrendered on the Fourth of July, 1863, thus appropriately celebrating the national holiday, that marks, as if with mile-stones, the progress of the Union. The thunder of artillery reverberated through the forests, followed by the ringing shouts of the victorious Federal troops. This sublime music proclaimed not only the doom of the defeated foe, but the joy of the whole North, because

> From the small crystal springs that were gleaming,
> Like gems in the green northern vales,
> To the gulf where the sunlight was streaming,
> In floods on the ocean-bound sails,
>
> The Father of Waters was sweeping
> Unvexed through the beautiful land;
> While Liberty, smiling and weeping,
> Rejoiced in the work of her hand.

The pine needles glittered and waved in the Southern breeze, upon which floated the banners that had been tattered and stained in this latest victory of freedom. A thousand mingling sounds seemed trying to drown the sweet rippling of the river, that still might be heard like a clear contralto softly joining its hymn of praise with the warlike symphony. .

From the bluffs about Vicksburg, a throng of pitiable men came pouring down, tottering with weakness, and within its now useless defenses, many lay dying of hunger and pain. The conquerors were generous to them, and the surgeons and nurses acted literally upon the Golden Rule; so, although that memorable day was marked by defeat to the Confederates, it brought the balm of peace and comfort to those who had suffered most.

The hospital tents were clean, airy places, supplied with comfortable cots, above which curtains and mosquito bars were suspended. Large palm leaf fans were supplied to all of the patients, and added greatly to their comfort. A considerable portion of the Federal Army was encamped in the vicinity of Vicksburg, for the purpose of rest during the midsummer heat. The soldiers were high-spirited and lively, and their quarters were comfortably and healthfully arranged, making an unusual amount of enjoyment possible to them. Few duties were required, and these were confined almost entirely to exercises which are agreeable to the true soldier. Many of the officers sent for their families to spend with them this unusual interval of peace and rest; and thoughts of home were suggested to many a brave fellow, by the sight of the fair and merry children who visited the camps. Often the gorgeous sunsets shed a glow of gold and crimson light upon a group of soldiers in their fresh uniforms, listening to the strains of some favorite air, played

softly by one of the regimental bands; and in the
short, dusky hour that followed, many longing eyes
gazed absently upon the brightening stars, while fancy
pictured, instead, the dear face of some one beloved,
now far away and lonely in her Northern home.

Though the soldiers were resting upon the laurels
which they had so dearly won, no link in the chain
of duty was broken, and the near future promised to
be full of hard service.   All through those quiet weeks
a thread of preparation for the autumn campaign was
woven.   Men from the hospital tents rejoined their
regiments, and as the season wore on, the numbers of
these increased daily, showing that amid those sunny
groves, faithful care and skill were unrelaxed, and
doing their priceless work.   Midsummer days and
sultry nights saw Mrs. Bickerdyke actively and constantly engaged in her chosen duties.   Patient toil
and much energy were required of her, and these were
not wanting.   Wherever she went, order and plenty
followed, as if invoked by some secret power.

The gentle zephyr, that brings health and pleasure,
excites little comment, though it may be highly appreciated; but the loud and sudden thunder-storm,
that purifies the air, is noticed near and far.   Thus it
may be attributed much to her commanding spirit
and dauntless courage in dealing with the few, whom
she found to be selfish and dishonest in regard to
sanitary work, that made her name become a familiar
and pleasant word to the officers and soldiers alike.
Her popularity served her well sometimes.   Upon
one occasion, an officer who had charge of sanitary

7

supplies was discovered by her in the act of making some perfidious use of them; and, as usual, was not permitted to pursue the course he had adopted. That he should be interfered with by her was more than his dignity could brook, and with all the pomp of offended authority, he complained to General Sherman.

"Who is she?" inquired the general.

"A Mother Bickerdyke," he scornfully replied.

"Oh! well," said the general, "she ranks me, you must apply to President Lincoln."

The disconcerted officer slunk quickly away, while the general indulged in a smile of amusement. Mrs. Bickerdyke was well known to him. He appreciated her remarkable abilities, and secured her services for his men, when the autumn campaign began.

Late in September the picturesque camp-life about Vicksburg was disturbed by the dictates of war. The tents were struck, and brigade after brigade marched away, their gleaming bayonets and bright uniforms enlivening every scene through which they passed. Sometimes their road wound through yellow corn fields, where the silken tassels nodded with promise in every breeze; and again it lay across plantations uncultivated and desolate, or between the hills and up the rivers, where echoes reveled in every note that rung through the sparse forests, from the moving hosts. Their steps were bent and their faces were turned towards Lookout Mountain to which their hearts leaped forward in anticipation of future conquests. The capture of Vicksburg shed a glory upon them, like that of the brilliant sunsets which foretold a fair and golden dawn. General Grant, the hero of this triumph, was still their guide, and every soldier looked with faith toward the star of his fame, that was rapidly ascending to the zenith of ultimate success. From border to border throughout the Union, his name was becoming synonymous with victory; and it inspired the armies with redoubled strength and courage.

The troops advanced by long and toilsome marches, with their eyes fixed upon the rainbow that seemed to encircle the clouded brow of Lookout Mountain; and in their train followed Mrs. Bickerdyke with General Sherman's lively and dauntless men.

As they proceeded eastward, the varying landscapes daily became more desolate. They had been ravaged by the conflicting armies, and autumn strove in vain to beautify them with the ruby and russet embroideries of her threadbare scarf. The dark blue outlines of Missionary Ridge, appearing against the sky, told Mrs. Bickerdyke that she had reached her destination. No welcome to a friendly fireside greeted her here, and offered rest after the long and wearisome journey; but instead, the field hospital near Chattanooga, with its gray tents, swept by chill winds, and filled with wounded soldiers, who needed her gentle care.

CHAPTER V.

DARK and grim appeared the craggy sides of Mount Lookout and Missionary Ridge, as the storms came sweeping around them, and whistling through the forest below. In these wind-swept woods, about three miles from Chattanooga, the field hospital for the men who had been wounded in the battle of Chickamauga, was located. Their frail tents, pitched among the trees, were often rent and overthrown by the gale; and sometimes giant boughs were hurled against them by the same pitiless force. Here the privations which the soldiers endured, were great. Supplies of all sorts were limited, and the approach of winter was heralded by the

(100)

bitter cold and dampness of a more than usually severe season. Although fuel could be obtained in
abundance from the forest, fires could not be arranged so as to give sufficient warmth. Around a
large "log-heap" of burning wood, placed in a small
clearing, several tents were pitched. Dark plumes of
smoke curled up from the blazing pile, and upon the
coals beneath, the frugal meals for the patients and
their attendants were prepared.

These "log-heaps" each with its circle of gray tents,
were numerous, forming a strange village, not unlike
those of the savage tribes, which had nestled about
the base of the same blue mountains long ago, when
the forests waved in primeval beauty, and the toma-
hawk and arrow were the weapons of war. Now instead. of these barbarous implements, the spirit of
battle looked upon the formidable array of artillery
frowning behind the entrenchments and fortifications
that scarred Mount Lookout's beetling brows, and the
stony sides of Missionary Ridge. Upon these natural strongholds the Confederate Army fancied itself
secure, and waited with confidence, while the Union
forces gathered in the surrounding valleys, and upon
the rolling hill-slopes, threaded by bright, silvery
rivers and streams, that only made the scene appear
darker and colder.

From the tents in the forest, a magnificent view of
these threatening heights could be obtained. The
panorama was remarkable for the bold grandeur of
nature seen in the rugged hills; and for the waving
flags and gleaming tents of the Southern hosts, that

appeared brilliant and clearly defined against the somber background. Mrs. Bickerdyke lost no precious time in contemplating this array of battle, but, with the force of an intensely practical nature, immediately began the work she found at hand. She selected a "log-heap," and, after enlarging it to double the size of the others, proceeded to prepare fresh and wholesome food, much of which was obtained from the stores that she had contrived to bring with her. Fragrant tea and coffee were made in the iron kettles upon the coals; and toast and broiled meat were prepared by means almost as rude and simple as that adopted by the gypsies. Delicious soup was kept steaming hot, and ready at all hours.

The soldiers had made little ovens for themselves of bricks and clay, and these suggested to Mrs. Bickerdyke the idea of having several of a larger size, constructed for her primitive kitchen. The plan was readily acted upon, and soon enabled her to prepare fine bread, roasted meat, and even cakes; so the distasteful "hard tack," which had been served so long, was replaced by fresh light bread, that many a grateful man declared equal to the appetizing loaves made in his own home.

The wildness and danger of their surroundings were never permitted to be absent from their minds. Constantly the rumble of wheels and the tramp of marching feet, the calls of the bugles and the beats of the drums, all, softened by distance, called up the vision of armed hosts rapidly preparing for battle; and not only this commotion kept them alert, but also the

deadly missiles that sped down from the mountain
slopes across the Union lines, threatening their refuge.

About three days before the battle, Mrs. Bickerdyke rejoined General Sherman's corps at the base of
Missionary Ridge.   She was received by many of the
soldiers with a true friendly welcome, which was to her
as gratifying as dew and sunshine are to a flower that
has been shut away from those grateful influences.
As yet no other woman had reached these scenes, and
being a stranger in an unfamiliar place, she felt the
want of sympathy that is so highly appreciated by a
warm and friendly nature.   The pleasant assurance
of thankful feelings and kind remembrances, which
was expressed by "the boys" for whom she had
toiled so earnestly during the hot summer at Vicksburg, was to her the reward most prized of any that
Providence could bestow.   In this, she   manifested
the true feminine spirit that actuated her to do and
dare so much for her country.   Although the soldiers
might call her "general," they felt that she was, in
truth, the "mother," about whose head filial eyes
could discern the matchless aureole that glorifies the
brow of motherhood.

The Battle in the Clouds began upon the 23d of
November, 1863, a threatening day in which autumn
scattered her hectic leaves upon the sod, and wept
and shivered in the gloom.   The mountain heights
revealed the fearful revelry of death which was proclaimed by the rolling thunder of artillery, and the
whistling of bullets.   Sometimes the white smoke
from long lines of rapidly discharged muskets as-

cended from the crags and defensive works; and
again it was puffed away in clouds from the booming
guns, making the power of war appear indeed most
terrible. From the almost deserted valley, Mrs.
Bickerdyke looked upon this sublime theater of
action far above her, scarcely discerning its magnificence; her heart was so full of hope and anxiety for
the valiant soldiers, who were bearing the old Union
flag steadily upward against the storm of fire and
lead that beat down their ranks. That first day of
the struggle was the most trying of all to her, because there was nothing to relieve the suspense which
it excited. During the dismal afternoon the wounded
were brought in from the fields of carnage, with faces
pale and streaked with powder, their uniforms tattered and stained with blood. The tents arranged
to receive them were pitched upon a small hill that
sloped down to the Tennessee River, at the base of
Missionary Ridge.

Night closed over the scene, dark and bitter cold;
and the wind blew out the lanterns and scattered the
fagots piled upon the "log-heaps." The roar of
artillery ceased to reverberate among the hills at
night-fall, and through the blackness that obscured
every surrounding object, the sighing of the winds in
the trees, and the murmuring of the river, came to
mingle with the groans of the wounded and dying.
Some of the tents were blown from their fastenings
by the gale, exposing the unfortunate sufferers, whom
they had sheltered, to indescribable agony. Here
even the matchless courage of the soldiers' mother

did not fail her. She hastened from tent to tent with medicine, dressings for wounds, and cordials. Burning coals and hot bricks were taken into the tents, and steaming beverages, administered freely, to counteract the fatal chills that insidiously crept over the men, when weakened from loss of blood and the fatigue of battle.

The skirts of Mrs. Bickerdyke's thick flannel dress were perforated as if by bullets, from being repeatedly set on fire by the coals and flying sparks of the "log-heaps," while she hastened about her duties. All through the night and during the day that followed, this work was continued. Wounded men swelled the number of the patients every hour, until night again mercifully arrested the work of death. But a new danger threatened them. The weather grew so cold that they were almost frozen; and Mrs. Bickerdyke hastened through the cutting blasts with glowing embers and hot bricks, until after midnight, when she became too much exhausted to continue this life-saving work any longer, and was compelled to take a few hours' rest.

On the 25th day of November the national flag floated from the purple summits of the mountains, that were· splashed with life-blood, bright as the red stripes in the folds of the glorious Union standard.

A few hours had changed the scene. On the day before, fleecy gray vapors had curtained from view General Hooker's intrepid men, as they scaled the dizzy heights of old Lookout. They had completely surprised the Confederates, driving them from their

rifle-pits; then, like an inspiration, came the order,
"Charge," and they sprang upward with resistless
fury, climbing the precipitous crags under the deadly
fire of the enemy, and never relaxing their efforts
until they had routed their antagonists, and carried
the whole position. This military feat, unrivaled for
brilliancy, was repeated the next day on Missionary
Ridge, when General Grant ordered an assault on
the whole Confederate line. It was pressed with
dauntless heroism, until the scorched and tattered
Union colors waved triumphantly above the crown
of the ridge, from which the Southern army fled in
disastrous confusion.

Now the clouds had dissolved in rain or drifted
away, and a clear azure sky permitted the sunshine
to gild and beautify every object of nature. It beamed
as brightly upon the stark figures of the unburied
slain as it did upon the Federal army, flushed with
the intoxication of victory. Although the men were
weary and almost overwhelmed with fatigue, they
still pursued their vanquished foes, who retreated
toward Ringold. There, on the 26th, an engagement
took place, which ended the four days' conflict, that
constituted one of the grandest and most terrible battles of the whole War of the Rebellion.   .

The men wounded at Ringold were sent to join
those near Chattanooga. Here, in the immense field
hospital, Mrs. Bickerdyke continued to labor, enduring the most severe hardships with remarkable resistance. As Christmas day approached, the good
cheer and joyful family gatherings, which make winter

holiday seasons so delightful, were painfully recalled by the disabled soldiers, because the dark foreboding present appeared even more wretched when contrasted with those memories. If holly and pine flourished in the woods about Chattanooga, they offered their treasures of scarlet berries an ı glossy tassels in vain; or perhaps they had been cut away by bullets and shells. Instead of sharing in festivities where music and light weave their spells of gladness about the altar and the fireside, the men lay in helpless pain. Sun-browned veterans of the war, in all the pride and vigor of perfect manhood, and slender boys whose frames were fired with youthful enthusiasm, had been struck and left helpless by cruel missiles and bayonets; and now the days that peace and pleasure claim saw many of them borne to their graves far from home, and interred with the brief yet impressive ceremonies of a military funeral.

A large number of these soldiers who were laid to rest at the foot of the mountains where they had fought and conquered so gloriously, were young, and their doom seemed the more to be regretted, because among them was many a youth,

> Within whose soul the gem of power
> Had promised to unfold,
> Into the glorious amaranth flower,
> Which is a rare immortal dower
> More precious far than gold.

> The laurels and the banners bright,
> The stars, and all the rest
> The future promised, sink from sight,
> When the young brow, so smooth and white,
> By Death's cold lip is pressed.

Ah! Fame and Freedom ne'er can know,
  When the young hearts are still,
What they have lost, beneath the snow
Of those pale brows—what laurels grow
  Unculled from vale and hill.

New Year's day was made one of gladness to Mrs. Bickerdyke, by the arrival of her cherished friend. Mrs. Porter. She had come from Cairo, which was the last place she had stopped at on her patriotic and charitable mission. Mrs. Bickerdyke welcomed her cordially, and at the same time indulged in a touching shower of tears that were a relief to her feelings, which had been severely taxed for weeks. Tears excite pity when shed by the young and helpless, but when they sparkle on the cheeks of one so strong and cheerful as Mrs. Bickerdyke, they call for the most sincere compassion, because they spring from sources so deep and difficult to reach.

These admirable companions pursued their work together, all through the hard, stormy winter and into early spring. Often food was supplied in what the poor sufferers tersely described as "starvation rations;" and at such times, these tender, self-sacrificing women divided their morsels with some young soldier who appeared weaker than the rest. Their respective characteristics here also led them to select different methods of performing their common tasks. In Mrs. Bickerdyke's nature, the inexhaustible warmth and hope made her presence a source of inspiration and courage that did more good than it is possible to estimate; while her compeer was as admirable, disseminating the influence of her pure, trustful faith, that enabled despairing men to bear the cross of their calamities.

Mrs. Porter distributed stores and nursed the sick, while Mrs. Bickerdyke continued to reign in her primitive kitchen, which was improved slowly, until it became of much importance. After a time, regular supplies of food and other stores were sent to the station at Chattanooga, and she frequently went in an army wagon, drawn by mules, to receive them. This was a tedious drive, over a rough and muddy road, rendered still more slow and wearisome on account of the bad condition of the mules. On her return to the hospital, she proceeded to do her usual day's work before taking any rest, baking bread and preparing other food until late at night. Though she sought her cot with weary steps and heavy eyes, a feeble moan always recalled her from her much-needed sleep to the side of the one in distress, and she saved many lives by this constant watchfulness.

In March, while the lingering storms continued to oss and drench the branches about their camp, the last of the convalescent soldiers were allowed to return on furlough to their Northern homes. There is something weird in the rapidity of change that frequently distinguishes great battles or calamities. But a single winter had passed over those mountains and valleys, and yet the events which had transpired during that time will render them forever haunted with associations of carnage, and sacred to the pages of history. Of the 80,000 Union men, whose uniforms had made the landscape blue in November,

none remained except those at rest under the sods,
which returning spring would soon cover with fresh
leaves and blossoms.

Mrs. Bickerdyke and Mrs. Porter went immediately
to Huntsville, and took charge of the military hospital there. Large numbers of the men who had suffered such terrible privations during the winter, were
afflicted with scurvy in consequence, and as varieties
of food necessary to their recovery could not be obtained in those ravaged and desolate regions of the
South, the two women decided to procure a supply
from the North. They started for Chicago, but on
reaching Nashville, their demands were satisfied for
the present; and they returned to the soldiers at
Huntsville, laden with vegetables and dried fruit, for
which the most sincere gratitude was shown.

Men, who had left congenial pursuits and the lux-
uries of a home; who had marched over the rocks and
marshes until their feet were bare, and their footprints
marked with blood; who had faced death in battle,
and defied the power of fever and cold, all for the
sake of their patriotism, received a pickled vegetable
or a morsel of dried fruit with trembling fingers, that
could not have been tempted to take a nugget of gold
in its place. This is not typical of the terrors of war,
like the field of conflict and the prison, but of the
privations incidental to active army life. Indeed, as
Carlyle says, " The historian should be a poet." No
one less gifted could do justice even to the heroes of
the ranks.

Later in the spring, the supply of fresh vegetables

again became inadequate, and Mrs. Bickerdyke went North to procure fruit and pickles. She found the people no less responsive to her requests than they had been the year before; yet, owing to the nature of the food required, she had to make greater personal efforts to obtain the desired amount. Upon many occasions she spoke in churches and at public meetings, making appeals remarkable for their directness and point, and for the success that followed them. While on this excursion, she observed with more interest the tender shoots appearing in the kitchen gardens, than the first bright rosebuds and pansies that ornamented many a porch and lawn. Her feelings were so deeply interested in the army work that she neglected this opportunity of taking a much-needed rest, in order to return to Huntsville as soon as possible. On reaching Nashville she received a gift of $100, to be used for the soldiers in any manner that she should deem most wise and beneficial. This had been sent by the people of Milwaukee. Her energy and earnestness had greatly impressed them while she was there upon her last visit, and, besides, they had not forgotten her remarkable " cow and hen mission."

She still devoted most of her services to the Army of the Tennessee; and her work was highly prized by all of the officers, from whom she received much consideration; now listening to General McPherson's offers to do anything in his power to assist her; and again, upon General Sherman's request, consenting to accompany his forces during the next campaign.

Early in March, 1864, General Grant was appointed

commander-in-chief of all the armies of the United States. This conferred upon him the power to control and direct no less than 700,000 Union soldiers, by whom he was honored and admired. After deciding upon the course he thought best to adopt, in order to crush the Rebellion, he gave General Sherman an important part of his plan to carry out. This was to move against Atlanta, which was held by the Confederate forces under General Johnston. With this design, General Sherman soon sent a thrill of excitement and preparation throughout the Federal camps at Chattanooga and Huntsville, where the greater part of his gathering army, now 100,000 strong, was stationed. For more than a month, the work of making all things ready for the military movements contemplated, went steadily on. When May arrived, with her sunshine and verdure, General Sherman was prepared to start with forces of which he said, " I doubt if any army ever went forth to battle with fewer *impedimenta,* and where the regular and necessary supplies of food, ammunition, and clothing were issued, as called for, so regularly and so well."

Like their leader, who set the example, every man forgot all personal considerations in his resolution to win the prize in view. Even the tents were left behind, both officers and men sleeping under the one dark, star-hung tent that night stretches over the hemisphere. They were full of determination and enthusiasm, and arose at dawn, shaking lightly the pearls of dew from their clothing, and beginning their duties with a jest or a snatch of song. During the first week in May, the army of General Sherman bent its steps toward the sea, well equipped to battle with the powerful foes, who were fortified in the cities and strongholds between.

Mrs. Bickerdyke and Mrs. Porter followed them, with their stores of all things necessary to alleviate the pain and lessen the trials of those who should become sick or wounded. Though they had seen and shared much suffering in sight of the beautiful mountains toward which their gaze was fixed in farewell, they advanced into the hostile country with hearts as fearless, and courage as great, as did any one in a blue uniform preceding them. Softer and dimmer grew the outlines of the peaks, until they appeared as if draped with folds of rich velvet, that had caught the luster of sunlight. That receding scene might well be panoplied with splendor, for there the laurels of triumph flourished, still fresh and bright with ruby gems of dew. Mrs. Bickerdyke was prepared for service. She was not carefully protected, although whatever was necessary to her comfort was supplied, as well as circumstances permitted. Besides, she was neither empty-handed nor at leisure. On reaching Ringold, where the railroad terminated, she was told that her sanitary supplies could not be sent further. Every means of transportation that the Government could utilize, was appropriated to its service, and at that time orders were issued to forward only necessary food, clothing, ammunition, and such things for the soldiers. Mrs. Bickerdyke did not submit to these stringent orders without making some effort to have

8

them changed.   Yet to do this, without much delay,
was difficult, as all the officers whose authority was
adequate to her purpose were many miles beyond.
While she was deliberating upon the dilemma, she
observed a train of mule teams, loaded with freight for
the army, about to start, and with characteristic determination resolved that her supplies should go with
it.   She went immediately to the master of transportation, who was familiar with the popular name of
Mother Bickerdyke, and succeeded in persuading him
to allow a small portion of her goods to be carried
upon each wagon.   By this means she was enabled
to convey everything that was necessary for immediate use to its destination.   Taking her seat in an ambulance, she was soon upon the road toward the
mountain defiles of Georgia.   It was well that she
lost but little time in Ringold, for ere the long day's
journey was at an end, the ominous roar of distant
cannon broke like a discord through the minor notes
of bird and insect life, that floated upon the evening
dusk.

She knew too well the meaning of those solemn
sounds, and her face grew pale, though her heart
leaped forward at the tidings.   The next morning
while all nature was resplendent with dew, glittering
in the clear light of May, she arrived at the battle-
field of Resaca.   Knapsacks and overcoats were piled
in little pyramids under the trees, and all about,
wounded men lay upon the sod, while the hospital
tents were being pitched.   One by one they were
borne into these hastily-arranged shelters, after

having had their wounds dressed by surgeons, whose operating tables were placed under wide-spreading trees, in the shade of which their duties were performed. Ghastly fragments of human bodies were piled upon the ground, and from this sickening sight, Mrs. Bickerdyke turned away to attend upon the pitiable beings who had suffered such losses.

Kneeling upon the ground, she bound up gaping wounds, and bathed agonized faces. She gave spirits and wine to those who were fainting, and thus labored until the field hospitals were made ready.

Then she appeared bustling about a rude, yet well-supplied kitchen, that seemed to have sprung into existence by means of such magic as that attributed to Aladdin's lamp. Nourishing food, so much needed by men in the prostrate condition of these soldiers, was given to them freely. To them it came as a token that even here they were within the reach of kindred and friends. It was manna from Heaven in the wilderness.

In a short time the patients were removed into the town of Resaca, now in possession of the Union soldiers, and placed in comfortable buildings, appropriated for military hospital purposes. Mrs. Bickerdyke remained at her post of duty here, while the valiant Federal forces were pursuing General Johnston's retreating army, and preparing for another battle. During this period, nurses arrived from the North, and the hospitals were completely organized. Well-arranged kitchens were prepared, and likewise fine laundries; so that proper food and clothing were supplied in abundance. This was accomplished principally through Mrs. Bickerdyke's enterprising spirit and ardent zeal, which always impressed those around her, and aroused in them similar qualities, if such were dormant. This faculty of discovering the latent powers of others, and the ability to incite them to action, gave every work in which she interested herself an impetus that greatly promoted its success.

When the army again attacked the Confederates, this noble woman was free to follow it into the field, and there minister to the wounded and dying, with the tenderness and efficiency that made her so widely known and so highly esteemed.

At Kingston, Georgia, Mrs. Bickerdyke labored in the hospitals, and there was much for her to do; as there were more than nine thousand disabled soldiers placed in them, and treated until they were able to travel to the more salubrious regions of the North. Early in the summer, many of the men, not being acclimated, were attacked with fever and sunstroke, and the cool, airy wards of the Kingston hospitals were, to such, havens of refuge most eagerly sought. When suffering from wounds, the light tent, or even the branches of trees arched into a shelter, may be quite comfortable and healthful for men accustomed to the atmospheric changes of all seasons, as the veterans were; but the burning agonies of fever and sunstroke, that seemed to make the strongest wither like a wilting plant, demand more careful treatment.

Through the bewildering sensations caused by feverish delirium, the only things that calm and soothe

the troubled nerves, are cooling potions and gentle
opiates, administered by the physician or nurse.   Mrs.
Bickerdyke's caution and pity enabled her to save a
noble young man from the most cruel neglect through
misapprehension.   Late one afternoon, a poor fellow,
in a soiled and dusty uniform, staggered to the door
and asked admittance in a thick and stuttering voice.
His congested face and entire appearance were mis-
taken for those of a drunken man, and he was ordered
to leave.   But Mrs. Bickerdyke's motherly heart re-
belled against this summary treatment.

"Let the poor boy have a chance to get over this
plight first," she remonstrated, and she soon had him
placed in a comfortable cot, when it was discovered
that he was suffering from sunstroke.   Prompt attention from the doctors, and faithful nursing, insured
his recovery.   If these had been withheld only a little longer, this young soldier, who proved to be a
most estimable man, would have been lost to his
friends and to his country.

In the early part of the season that dreaded army
disease, the scurvy, made its appearance, and demanded special treatment.   The wagon trains and
railroads were taxed to their uttermost capacity, and
yet could not transport sufficient quantities of vegetables to supply the soldiers.   Later, when summer's
fervid sunbeams had dissolved the mists and filled the
woodlands with wild fruit and flowers, the disorder
disappeared.   On the banks of the streams grew
clumps of thorny blackberry bushes, and the soldiers
sought them as eagerly as school-boys, for the sprays

that bent down to the very water's brink with the
weight of sweet, ripe berries. Broad fields of corn
next offered roasting ears, thickly set with plump,
milky kernels; and after this the army had an abundance of such food.

The dense woods that mantled the rough and un-
frequented vales and ridges stretching southeast to
Atlanta, were filled with the soldiers of both the
Northern and Southern armies. The Confederate
columns were constantly driven from stronghold to
stronghold while the boys in blue advanced. But
every foot of the ground they gained, was hotly dis-
puted and dearly won. Rocks and trees, hastily
thrown up embankments of earth, and every species
of cover available, served as shelters from which the
contending armies fought in a continuous battle,
waged by strong skirmish lines that often stretched
across ten miles of the rugged creek-veined country.
The sounds of musketry and artillery tortured the
air every hour, for night stayed not the soldiers'
hands. It was a strange and terrible warfare. Only
glimpses of each other from behind the formidable
defenses could the opposing soldiers obtain; and these
were frequently as mysterious and uncertain as the
delusive objects glimmering in a *mirage.*

Through the centuries long gone by, savages waged
their barbarous wars within those woodlands. The
startling Indian whoop and whir of arrows sounded
through the stately vistas, in which the painted combatants may have appeared to each other and van-
ished again, with the impish uncertainty characteristic

of their wild and cruel natures. Now their bones lay crumbling within the mounds that rise upon the banks of the Etowah River, murmuring through the glades at no great distance. The race which drove them from their battle-grounds now pursue upon the same fields as fierce a strife, in somewhat the same manner, yet far more deadly and grand; for these warriors vastly outnumber the red men who fought, and they are superbly equipped with weapons of terrific might, perfected by the art and science of all ages. Their formidable trenches wrinkle the ground, and their charges are unrivaled in either boldness or strategy.

On toward Dallas, our forces pressed through the dense woods, over the sharp ridges, across the streams, and along the winding, rut-seamed wagon roads, that converged toward the Confederate strongholds. · At the place called "New Hope," from the church of that name, which held its spire aloft among the trees that fringed the cross-roads there, a spirited engagement took place. It began late in the afternoon, on the 25th of May. The fighting was continued until night was far advanced, when from the black storm clouds, lowering in the heavens, heavy rains fell, putting an end to the conflict; but the next day it was recommenced, and raged throughout the week. During this time so much suffering was endured, and so many fell killed or wounded, that the soldiers called the place "Hell Hole."

Men were borne to the rear constantly, and soon a vast field hospital appeared in the woods, but a short

distance from the line of battle. Thousands were
gathered here, as the prolonged and cruel strife was
continued. Some were carried through the rain, and
left upon the muddy ground, in their splashed and
dripping garments, to await the attention of the surgeons, who were greatly overworked. The discom-
forts and difficulties occasioned by the storms, caused
delays and sickness, adding to the terrors and dis-
asters to which the soldiers were subjected, and re-
tarding the progress of their exciting victories. Still
burning with the thirst for triumph, each man did
valiantly his part, and often won a palm of glory for
some daring feat; or perhaps sheathed within his
quivering flesh, a missile that laid him low with the
wounded and dying.

One of the latter, whose experience may serve as a
prototype for many, was in ambush behind a cluster
of tall ferns and shrubbery, through which he had succeeded in sending several bullets into the brown
homespun of more than one Southerner. Growing
less cautious, as the glow of excitement pervaded his
being, he straightened his tall figure for a moment so
that he became visible to some one of the enemy, concealed in the woods before him. In an instant he
heard the whiz of a bullet, then of several, and felt a
sting across his cheek and along his arm, as if a whip
lash had struck him. The world grew dark as he
dropped upon the ground, and he felt his own warm
blood in his eyes and upon his hands, as he tried to
clear his vision. When consciousness returned, dim
slanting raindrops beating into his face, and through

the trees, gave his surroundings the weird character of a dream. Wounded men were lying upon the grass all about him, and a few soldiers and negroes were removing these as rapidly as possible. His turn came, and soon he was placed upon the table in a surgeon's tent, where again unconsciousness mercifully conquered pain with oblivion. His arm was amputated; then followed weary days, during which he slowly recovered from his injuries. Mrs. Bickerdyke came through the rain to his tent with bread and wine. Drops of water trembled like beads upon her hood, and her dress was damp and mudsplashed, still her voice rang pleasantly, and her words were patient and kind, as though she felt no discomfort. Fever soon set in, and for a long time he lingered upon the verge of death. Through the painful wanderings of delirium, the knowledge of her watchful care, and faith in her skill, seemed to sustain him, and when the fever left him, though faint and exhausted, he recognized in her face the maternal love and devotion that had been the means of saving his life. Thus she labored here in much the same manner that had distinguished her course amid the painful scenes through which she had previously passed. Besides, the experience gleaned from those fields, facilitated the progress of every branch of her work here.

After preparing all of the delicacies that could be obtained, as well as wholesome food of an ordinary nature, she spent the hours in which she might have rested, at the side of some feeble and suffering soldier.

Enough cannot be said in praise of the good her encouraging words and cheerful presence did those who
came within her sphere of action. She was often
told that her care was more potent to cure than medicine; and being so strong and energetic, she visited
the thousands around her almost daily. Much leisure
for this purpose was gained through her magnetic
influence over all whom she assumed to command.
A small force of negroes went and came at her bid-
ding, as if magnetized by her will; and convalescent
patients delighted to show their gratitude by un-
wearying efforts in her service. She directed those
about her so naturally and gracefully, that obedience
to her wishes seemed offered rather than exacted.
Like others gifted with a faculty of commanding, she
could attend to a variety of details with rapidity and
success.

Every day five hundred loaves of light, delicious
bread were baked under her supervision. She peeped
into the jars of foamy yeast to ascertain if it was exactly right, and never failed to examine the dough
while rising. Passing her hand rapidly along the
warm, smooth loaves, she could tell with the exactness
gained from experience when they were ready for
the oven; and the dusky members of her devoted
retinue credited her with witch-like powers, declaring
that if she did not "try the dough the bread was
sure to be bad."

No interruption was occasioned to her bakery, by
the removal of a hospital, or when traveling was necessary. The dough was set to rise, and kept warm by

means of blankets, while being moved in the wagons. At evening it was baked as usual. This was
accomplished by means of a portable oven which the
soldiers had prepared of bricks, each one being in-
geniously numbered, so that the oven could be readily taken apart or put together. From early dawn
until long after night-fall, roaring fires burned red in
the wide fire-place attached to it. Mrs. Bickerdyke
arranged in these woods a laundry, somewhat resembling that which she had superintended at Corinth,
and the negroes, under her direction, performed a
prodigious amount of work here, and in the gypsy-
like kitchen.

The purpose for which she accompanied General
Sherman's army was successfully accomplished, for
the wholesome food and clean clothing she thus supplied in the midst of the wilderness, assisted greatly
in saving the lives of the sick and wounded; and besides, the charm of her powers, diffused even about
this wild habitation of pain, something of home-like
comfort and celestial peace.

CHAPTER VI.

NWARD swept the conquering army, driving the Confederates from their fortified positions. Cassville, Allatoona, and Dallas were taken, one by one, during the latter part of May, and the first days of June found the Union soldiers strong and ambitious, and still advancing against their foes, who had retreated to the famous heights of Kenesaw Mountain. Although so glorious, the costs of their triumphs demand a tear, for besides the vast numbers who had been left sleeping their last sleep in the lonely, ravaged woodlands, no less than 13,000 had been wounded, and most of

(124)

these lay languishing in the rude tents of the field hospitals, still within hearing of the ceaseless sounds of battle.

The early summer was not distinguished by balmy weather and blue skies, such as usually render that season so delightful, yet little restraint was imposed upon the progress of victory. Ere the Fourth of July permitted every loyal heart to swell with the joy of again celebrating the anniversary of our national independence, the star-spangled banner floated upon the peaks of Kenesaw and Lost Mountains, planted there by the gallant Federal soldiers. They had also captured Marietta, and were pursuing their antagonists southward toward the Chattahoochee River.

While the weeks were passing, the scenes by which Mrs. Bickerdyke was surrounded became more painful and trying every day. Sunstroke and fever added their victims to the many who were brought wounded to the tents and buildings used as hospitals. A large number were sent to their homes and to various military hospitals in the North, as soon as they could be moved with safety; but so continuous and fierce were the conflicts at the front, that the labors of the surgeons and nurses, engaged in the field hospitals, were not diminished.

At Marietta Mrs. Bickerdyke assisted in organizing a hospital large enough to accommodate 1,800 wounded men, who were lying upon the ground, exposed to the burning summer heats, and malarial night dews. Dr. A. Goslin, late surgeon 48th Illinois Volunteers, who had charge of this, the 15th A. C.

field hospital, says: "Her services were simply indispensable. I could not have conducted it without her."

Here two very interesting patients were placed under her care. They had been nick-named "the twins," because their friendship was so remarkably deep; and also, "the babies," on account of their extremely helpless condition. One had lost his leg, and the other was stricken with fever. Side by side they lay in their narrow cots, offering mutual comfort and assistance, in a manner so feeble and weak that the sight was most pathetic. It appealed strongly to Mrs. Bickerdyke's maternal sympathies, and she became indeed a mother to the "poor, helpless boys," as she called them. Their youthful faces, so pitifully thin and worn from suffering, beamed with smiles at her approach, and "Mother Bickerdyke" was constantly among the words which they murmured to each other.

Nelson Hemplemen, the one afflicted with fever, succumbed to the disease, dying like some flower cut off by that Southern blight, which destroyed so many in those terrible summers of the war. The other, whose name was J. S. Eastwood, recovered through Mrs. Bickerdyke's tender devotion, which had also soothed his comrade during wearisome days of pain, to the very hour of his death. Mr. Eastwood's gratitude to her knew no bounds, and through all the years that have come and gone since, he has remained one of her most sincere friends. He describes some of her noble self-sacrifices enthusiastically:—

" I have known Mother Bickerdyke to come to our ward long after midnight, for the purpose of relieving a suffering soldier who was bleeding to death while the doctors and nurses were wrapt in slumber. They drew their pay whether awake or asleep, so would sleep on unless called, but she was ever alert to catch the faintest sound of distress, and to her timely efforts many of my comrades are indebted for their lives."

The wonderful oven, the great laundry, and the brave, cheerful woman who presided over them, besides nursing as many of the sick and wounded as though she did nothing else, became more widely known and appreciated every day. A soldier could not be met who had neither seen nor heard of Mother Bickerdyke. She was in the midst of her duties, and still they kept accumulating around her in such multitudes that one less courageous would have been dismayed.

Across the landscapes glimmering in the heat, the frowning defenses of Atlanta were seen. General Sherman's valiant soldiers, determined to take this "Gate City of the South," besieged it night and day. Shells and balls were poured into the streets without intermission, and the buildings frequently catching fire, blackened the sultry air with clouds of smoke that seemed ominous of its doom.

The field hospital in the vicinity covered thirty acres of ground, and sheltered thousands of sick and wounded men. Throughout the long summer, from dawn, when the blazing day-star made every cloud blush and disappear, to the sunset hour, others still were brought in to increase the lists of patients, and swell the cares of those who attended upon them. Faithful watchers grew tired and faint at their duty, through the long, oppressive heat of day, which was diminished so little by the coming of night, that the difference was scarcely perceptible. Yet Mrs. Bickerdyke was able to continue her work with unflagging energy. The good she did can never be fully known, nor adequately r warded, for she saved to the Government not only thousands of dollars, but the lives of many brave soldiers. What she restored to yearning and waiting hearts, and to whom she preserved the joy of life and health, only the countless numbers who possess these blessings through her toil and self-sacrifice can estimate.

It would be fruitless to attempt a description of all that is worthy of note in her devotion to the private soldiers; and the past proves that she was as constant and faithful in her labors for the officers as she was to her favorites.

A young corporal, Alvin Wait, of Company D, 127th Illinois Volunteers Infantry, may be remembered as one whose life she saved at Marietta. He was placed in a ward appropriated to those who were mortally wounded. This promising young man of twenty years lay crushed and half unconscious, awaiting only the relief which death brings, when Mrs. Bickerdyke came to him, and applied every means of healing known to her skill. Recollections of her are clearly defined among the misty visions which connect themselves with the hours of agony he endured there. Her kind face came and went like that of some visitant from the realms of hope and peace, bringing with her the life-giving essence of her native climes. She was untiring in her efforts to relieve the sufferings of even those who had been marked by the destroying angel for his own, and, as in this instance, she often snatched, before his sweeping sickle fell, what others had deemed impossible to save from his garner.

A detailed description of interesting scenes and occurrences that took place in these abodes of suffering, would fill volumes. The most quaint and romantic circumstances arose to engage the attention of those who might be observant of such things; while others were so sad and terrible that tears wrung from the very heart's core seemed vain emblems of the sorrow which they only half expressed. Although Mrs. Bickerdyke witnessed these cruel sights day in and day out through continuous months, she never became hardened in the least with regard to them. Her sympathies were always as delicately sensitive to the pathetic and touching incidents constantly arising, as though they had been rare, and those tender chords that vibrate in response to another's woe, seldom awakened.

The 22d of July was distinguished by the battle of Atlanta. Strong Confederate forces attacked boldly and repeatedly the Army of the Tennessee, then commanded by General McPherson. During the conflict, which lasted from noon until late in the sul-

try summer night, the fighting was fierce, and the
slaughter terrible. This engagement resulted in a
repulse of the enemy, but victory was gained at a
fearful cost. General McPherson, who was one of
the most noble and highly admired men in the Union
Army, was killed while riding at some distance ahead
of his staff and orderlies. He was passing through a
dense grove and coming suddenly upon an ambus-
cade of the enemy was shot dead. Beside this loss,
hundreds of brave soldiers fell, following their leader
fearlessly into the " valley of the shadow."

General Logan who assumed command of the
Army of the Tennessee, was fully competent to perform the responsible duties thus suddenly thrust upon
him; and as this army fought the battle almost un-
aided, the victory was to him a gallantly-won laurel
set with glory which adds greatly to the luster of his
fame. While he was pressing on to triumph in the
field of action, the promising young General McPherson lay cold and still upon a rude bier in the Howard
House. But here no solemn hush prevailed out of
respect to the presence of the honored dead, for many
shots from the scene of strife struck the building and
threatened its destruction. For this reason General
Sherman ordered the body to be taken for immediate safety to the hospital, and so it became Mrs.
Bickerdyke's duty to compose the handsome features
of this young man thus cruelly blasted by death in
the splendor of his prime.

Gently she closed his eyes in his last sleep. Her
pity went forth to that mother so soon to be stricken

with grief. With thoughtful tenderness she selected some relic which she knew would be treasured by one who had loved him so fondly. The coat he had worn was pierced by the ball that had taken his life, and was stained with his heart's blood; so she washed it with her own hands and sent it with a message to his bereaved mother by a soldier who was going directly to her home in Clyde, Ohio.

In the autumn, General Sherman decided to sever all connection with his base and undertake the grand march to the sea. Extraordinary efforts were made to select for this expedition only such soldiers as were able-bodied, experienced, and capable of vigorous action. The sick and wounded were sent to Chattanooga and to other military hospitals further north, or to their homes. Mrs. Bickerdyke remained upon the scene of her labors until the very night of the evacuation of Atlanta by the Union army. Trees and intervening hills shut away from her view the hideous sight of its destruction; yet the sounds of bursting shells came faintly to her ears, recalling the conflicts that had raged there all through the sultry summer; and a glare of lurid light fringed the horizon in its direction with an angry line of red. Above the smouldering ruins a huge column of black smoke hung like a pall, and thus the doomed city faded from view. Those who had conquered and crushed it marched on with shouts and martial music. Mingling with these spirited strains, the voices of 60,000 veterans swelled in the measures of their favorite battle songs. The strong and thrilling notes reverberated

through the hills of Georgia, as the legion swept
on, feasting upon the garnered stores of their foes,
whose bosoms they filled with terror and dismay.

Away from the forests and cities, marked by the
devastation of war, Mrs. Bickerdyke traveled, her
mind still busy with plans for the future. She had
grown thin, and her countenance revealed less of
freshness and color than perfect health always gives.
The hard and wearing toils and the desperate scenes
of strife which had so lately marked her experience
already began to slumber in her memory with the
softened and dissolving outlines that characterize
dreams. Clear sunlight and the bracing Northern air,
sharp and pure with the breath of autumnal frost,
gave her an undefined feeling of exhilaration, which
made the prospect before her seem one brilliant vision
of promise.

She went to Philadelphia where she obtained large
supplies of sanitary goods, and to numerous smaller
cities for the purpose of collecting still more. These
she distributed to soldiers in military hospitals, and
to those in winter quarters who were frequently as
much in want of them as the helpless sufferers lying
in hospital wards.

The first great Sanitary Fair, held in Chicago, during the fall of 1863, had been discussed in every paper
and periodical. It had awakened enthusiasm throughout the whole North, for its success had resulted in
larger benefits to the sanitary cause, than even its
most sanguine well-wishers had anticipated. Contributions had poured in from places far and near all

over the Union. The procession that had formed to deliver gifts on the opening day was estimated to be over three miles in length.

Rare and priceless treasures were lent for the adornment of this fair, and the numerous others that followed it, making the departments unique and fascinating with a splendor that might rival the oriental magnificence of a Turkish palace. All that the most successful business ability, and woman's matchless power, could do, was done to promote the success of this patriotic undertaking.

The gift which perhaps was the most remarkable and far reaching in its results was the original draught of the Proclamation of Emancipation from President Lincoln. This precious document, bestowed by that hand which was always stretched forth in behalf of justice and humanity, was sold for $3,000. A worthy use was made of this sum, for it proved to be a golden magnet that soon attracted to itself enough to build the Home for Illinois soldiers.

By means of this fair the marvelous sum of nearly $100,000 was obtained, to be distributed through the Northwestern Branch of the Sanitary Commission. Besides, it proved a conspicuous example, which prompted efforts of the same kind in countless other places, where the fairs were upon a scale in keeping with the number of the inhabitants, and the amount of good done by them was large. In this way a pleasant source of profit was made the means of recreation that could be enjoyed with sentiments of charity and patriotism.

Mrs. Bickerdyke was very influential in assisting and stimulating the people who made efforts of this kind to serve our country. Little fairs were held in church parlors, and in appropriate halls hired for the purpose. Young girls, in their costumes of bright wool, wore picturesque aprons of lawn and lace, tied with coquettish bows, knotted of ribbons of red, white, and blue. They brought cups of fragrant coffee about upon trays, in the center of which were piled pyramids of delicious sandwiches and crisp cakes. Offering these refreshments to the guests, they accumulated little heaps of small change in the place of their dainties. The fair tables were attractive on these occasions, being decorated with flags, and covered with an indescribable mass of useful and ornamental things, but the pretty girl who dealt in these articles seemed to influence trade more than her wares. Like the English beauty who sold a rose for a sovereign, the maid at a table often held out some brilliant scarf or soft handkerchief, and obtained for it ten times as much as its intrinsic value. Perhaps her winning smile, or sweetly expressed explanation as to the object of its price, opened the purse strings of some penurious old person who would not have thought of buying under other circumstances.

Many leisure hours and long evenings were spent by active young girls in preparing salable articles for these fairs. Afternoons were passed by little companies of them, engaged upon the same kind of work, and when a fair was held, their blooming faces and joyous spirits contributed not a little to the success of the enterprise. Here, at least, all fun-loving beings found a welcome, and they held high carnival. Shining coins and crumpled notes slipped through their rosy fingers, giving them as much pleasure, apparently, as though designed for symbols of their innocent witchery, as well as the hard-earned price of their generous work. If the boys who wore the blue could have known how enthusiastic were those patriotic women to help and comfort them amid their hardships, it would have brightened many a dark hour with pleasurable thoughts. Gain for them was to these merry girls the cap sheaf of success. The fairest one among them, however bright her glance and captivating her smile, could scarcely compete with Mother Bickerdyke in this vivacious and good-natured rivalry. Her fame was a spell which few could resist, and if it did not prove the "open sesame" to noble and generous sentiments, her stirring words, and the sight of her countenance, animated with earnest and cheerful expressions, obtained what other influences failed to procure. By some mysterious means, she always possessed a reserve store of whatever was necessary in her work, and so never lost an opportunity of helping those who needed her aid.

Winter came, and the frost sprites wrought their usual change in the landscapes, covering them with a mantle as pure and light as ermine, and by their elfish strategems, driving every one to the glowing fireside. Mingled with the enchanting fairy tales and legendary lore, which the holiday season revives each

year with a never-failing charm, came rumors of
General Sherman's march to the sea. The dazzling
imagery of the Arabian Nights, made real in the
heart of the new world, could scarcely entrance those
who might listen to accounts of the wonder, with a
more engrossing interest than did the news of this
triumphant expedition.

The march through Georgia was a grand success;
and the city of Savannah, looking out on the blue
waters of the broad Atlantic, was in possession of
the gallant United States soldiers. Union anthems
echoed through the streets, and the stars and stripes
of the national ensign waved once more on the
Southern breeze.

The news of these victories were received by Mrs.
Bickerdyke as messages inviting her again to her
chosen fields. She went immediately to New York,
and from thence sailed for the South, where, amid
the stately groves and broad savannas of an unfriendly
land, brave men were languishing in hospitals and
prisons. Her helpful hand was stretched out to them
amid these unfamiliar scenes, and on this account was
thrice welcome. Drizzling rains swept up from the
sea, and made the long, green moss that clung to the
aged oaks, seem like tattered and tear-stained crape.
How different was this from the prairies and forests
which she had left, all crisp and sparkling with mill-
ions of crystalline frost heads and glittering icicles!
The joys of home and fond companionship she had
exchanged for the gloomy hospital wards, which were
her dwelling-places; but homesick feelings were soon

dispersed by the grateful words and looks of those to whom she ministered. Besides, her motive, the same as theirs, was to assist in conquering the Rebellion.

At Wilmington she took care of a large number of Union soldiers who had been rescued from Andersonville and Florence prisons. The fearful sufferings of the captives at Andersonville have been so graphically described, that to recount their misfortunes or delineate their horrible tr als, seems an unnecessary task. Men, weakened in body from starvation and confinement in a noisome atmosphere, become as much altered in their minds and dispositions as they are physically changed. They grow as fretful and peevish as little children, and lose all idea of the relative importance of things. When hungry and weary, Esau exchanged his birthright for a mess of pottage; and, like him, they frequently attribute value to what is of little importance, while the ruling aims of life may be lost sight of altogether. Considering this, it is remarkable, that so few forgot the exalted motives that made them don the blue and follow their country's flag into the perils of civil warfare. Though tempted by such invitations and bribes as they were least able to withstand, they continued to sink in weakness and pain with the jewel of honor still bright and untarnished upon their bosoms.

Professor John G. Lemmon, formerly of the 1st Michigan Cavalry, and who has since become noted as a botanist in California, was one of the 11,000 Union soldiers confined in Florence Prison, South Carolina. He pictures the woes that fell to their lot as only one who has shared such misery could. The crowded and half-starved men were entirely exposed to the weather, and often had to pace all night the narrow limits of the space to which they were restrained, to keep from freezing.

A description of their ragged and soiled garments, of their poor mud hovels, and of their scanty food, makes a painful story indeed; but the most cruel features of their misfortunes were the tauntings and temptations to which they were subjected. Their jailers came to them each day with such words as these:—

"Are you hungry? Look at me, and say whether you would like to eat such food as I do or not? Are you cold? Look at my warm clothes and tell me how a rig of this kind would suit you? Outside the gates the air is sweet and fresh; and there is plenty to eat and to wear. Only take the oath of allegiance to the Confederacy, and freedom is yours."

He who could not be enticed by such allurements, when so miserably reduced in all temporal conditions, as these men were, is truly like gold that has been tried in the fire.

Among such sufferers, weak and emaciated in body, and feeble in mind, so far as petty annoyances were concerned, Mrs. Bickerdyke was a pillar of strength. Besides she moved among them like a mother, regarding as tenderly their fretful desires, and responding as patiently to their groundless complaints.

General Sherman's army was moving northward through the Carolinas, while the cities trembled at its approach. Penetrating drizzles kept the ground muddy, and made the air damp and unhealthful; yet the soldiers advanced rapidly. Day after day Kilpatrick's daring cavalry and a strong skirmish line, protected warily the moving legions from surprise. The army baffled the Confederates in every attempt made to retard or check their progress. Dense jungles, watery marshes, and swollen rivers, all intercepted their chosen pathway; but the obstacles which nature placed before them, were overcome as successfully as those interposed by the stubborn and despairing enemy. Flooded swamps and treacherous quicksands were impotent to hinder them from reaching the guarded cities, and fortified camps; and when these places were approached, the Southern armies were unable to hold them against such irresistible forces. The Union artillery and musketry poured forth their iron and leaden hail only at the command of victory; and the sulphurous fire and smoke rose ever as incense to the triumphant republic.

Beaufort, which was taken by General Sherman in the early part of February, 1865, received many of the Federal soldiers, who were wounded or disabled; and to this place Mrs. Bickerdyke came from Wilmington. She took charge of one of the largest military hospitals that the place contained; and here her usual routine of labor was pursued, blessing those who occupied the numerous wards. Situated in the midst of a hostile people, as they were, groundless rumors and false excitements penetrated even the hospitals. Mrs. Bickerdyke's commanding presence could immediately soothe the agitation of all the patients under her charge. Every thought she gave to them, and she seemed possessed of the power of an enchantress when it was necessary to meet any peril or emergency. She remained here until she had accomplished a vast amount of work. Only a short time was she permitted to enjoy the results of her achievements; for the dark pines and overflowing rivers in the vicinity of Beaufort had not yet begun to show the influence of approaching spring, when she was again called to new and different scenes.

General Sherman, with his army, had been engaged about Columbia and Cheraw, where daring feats and decisive victories made his course brilliant. He took possession of these places, and advanced on Fayetteville and Goldsboro'.

The battle of Averysboro' was fought on the 15th and 16th days of March, 1865. Heavy rains fell until the battle was nearly ended. After nightfall, upon the 16th, the Confederates, under General Hardee, retreated from the field. Strewn promiscuously over the wet and bloody ground, the Northern and Southern soldiers lay side by side. All surgical operations necessary were performed by surgeons of the Union army, for the injured men who had fallen from the enemy's ranks, and who had been deserted by their vanquished comrades. Nearly 500 of the victors had received wounds, and they were placed in ambulances that accompanied the army trains. The United States forces were marching on toward their objective point, which was Goldsboro.'

Upon the 19th of March, General Johnston's army was met near Bentonville, and an engagement took place, resembling, in most particulars, that of Averysboro'—even to the rain, which poured down upon the combatants; yet the fighting here was much heavier, and when the Confederates beat their retreat, there were more than 1,000 Union soldiers wounded. These were taken to Goldsboro' by the veterans, who could now enter, without further resistance, the captured city.

Mrs. Bickerdyke followed the army, stopping wherever the wounded were left, and doing for them what she had done for innumerable soldiers since the fall of Sumter called the people of the United States to arms. Through the sunny air of returning spring came harbingers of peace. The gloomy war clouds were rifted here and there, and dazzling rainbows arched over the dark and blood-stained regions that had been subdued by the conquerors.

Although the soldiers under General Sherman had just finished a march of more than 400 miles, the distance which they had traversed since leaving Savannah, and though many battles had been fought and swollen rivers crossed in wintry weather, they were strong and well, seeming to have had much keen and exciting enjoyment. Now and then the lively voice of some soldier whom Mrs. Bickerdyke had met before, would greet her heartily. Then he would proceed to interest her with a friendly account of the adventures which had befallen him since leaving Atlanta. Among the most interesting were the ludicrous anecdotes related of the "bummers." Much curiosity had been excited about them, by reports received through the Southern press, some of which were true, while others were slanderous, or altogether fictitious. To Sherman's armies these men were very useful all along the course of their famous marches.

When the anxious North had supposed the invaders to be starving, these jovial men had been resorting to all sorts of devices in order to collect food and forage. In little companies they left their regiments at dawn, and usually returned before dark, mounted upon horses, loaded with provisions of every kind. The army was well supplied, so that, in this respect, the expedition resembled a prolonged picnic. Delicious hams and fat turkeys were not rare; and they were none the less palatable from having been cooked over a bivouac fire, after a long day's march in the wintry air.

Kilpatrick's cavalrymen also had most interesting incidents to relate. The men mounted their horses and sped over the roads fearlessly, although they were subjected to constant perils, being so much feared and detested by the population of the South. But to General Sherman, these gallant riders were valuable beyond measure. Many a Southern housewife has seen her store of ham and flour, which she had concealed with so much art and toil in secret places, discovered as readily by these foragers as if they knew from instinct where such things were to be found. The articles were taken to supply the army, or destroyed before her eyes, if it was not possible to carry them away.

Frequently while riding gaily along in the woods, · a rifle ball would come whistling through the branches from a marksman hidden at no great distance. If it chanced to miss them all, they would put spurs to their horses' sides and soon be out of range. Surprising and destroying the Confederate wagon trains was also a lively and hazardous part of their duties; for the sturdy drivers sometimes made a desperate attempt to defend the property in their charge.

There was so much enterprise and action in those stirring times that every day was crowded with events. The gallant horsemen soon acquired a taste for adventure, and were proud of their position. They moved rapidly from point to point, performing feats of daring that kept them constantly filled with excitement. Now they scattered along a river course to find a suitable place for the engineers to lay their pontoon bridges; and next they dashed down upon a mountain pass and seized it for the army.

A crisis was approaching in the campaign of the Carolinas. General Grant with his powerful legions was pressing the Confederate leader, Lee, to his last resources; and it was thought that he would join General Johnston's shattered and discouraged columns in North Carolina, and, thus strengthened, turn upon General Sherman's forces. Great excitement prevailed among the latter while they were making ready for a final struggle. Soon the army was in a superb condition. The infantry were noticeable for their bright uniforms and shining bayonets; the cavalry, for their sleek and glossy charges; and the officers were splendid with their new and brilliant trappings.

An unusual tone of gaiety began to steal over the entire army. Comrades seemed to realize for the first time that the grim spirit of war was vanishing from the land, like mist before the morning sunbeams; and, with light hearts, they gathered around the bivouac fires, discussing the terrible past and the brightening future, with unwonted zest. The conflict supposed to be approaching was so uncertain that it only added a keen interest to the present, leaving out that poignant suspense which steals into the secret recesses of every heart on the eve of battle. All mirth had a genuine ring in it, such as before had been a rarity. The friends whom Mrs. Bickerdyke had won sought her persistently, and told her, with untiring interest, of their homes and future plans. To such disclosures she listened with a willingness that was more than courteous, for it displayed as beautifully her deep maternal love for those brave young veterans as did her midnight watches over them when they had lain wounded in frail hospital tents.

Her countenance was often radiant with bright and spirited expressions, while she joined in the merriment of lively groups, that delighted to interest her with their jovial amusements.

Some soldiers in fresh uniforms, bright with burnished buttons, waited upon her one sunny morning, and tendered her a review. She donned her bonnet with a smile, and permitted herself to be stationed in an elevated and suitable place. Then the fine old cows, which had supplied them with milk, filed past her. Each one had been curried until her coat was as smooth and glossy as satin.

Their horns fairly glittered from being polished, and their hoofs had been blackened and brushed until they were as bright as patent leather. The favorites were decked with little flags, and a lively march was played as the queer ranks moved along, with now and then a mellow low, and a restive break in the lines, made by some mild-eyed creature that appeared to delight in keeping to herself the constant attention of the jolly veterans.

Many of these cows had traveled a great distance with the army. All the way along the marches from Atlanta, cattle had been taken from their native pastures and driven with the provision trains to supply milk and beef. The fine, gentle milch cows were a treasure to Mrs. Bickerdyke, enabling her to make custards and such delicacies for the patients, at times when it would have been impossible to obtain appetizing food for them, and this boyish prank, the *cows' review*, was a pleasant tribute, which she greatly enjoyed.

The eyes of friends did not look upon her always with the twinkling glance of mirth, or the earnest expression of those who sought her sympathy. Many discerned the altered and careworn look, which was most noticeable upon her countenance when her features were in repose. Silvery gleams of gray were far more numerous in her heavy hair than they had been

10

a few short seasons ago. A peculiar curve had been wrought in her cheek and lip by her long association with the wounded and dying.

> She had looked on death in the crimsoned field,
>   Where the soldiers lay as they fell.
> 'Neath clouds of sulphurous smoke she had kneeled
>   On fragments of splintered shell;
>
> And the scene had lent to her cheerful face,
>   An expression new and grave,
> Which had given to it the lines of grace,
>   That beautify the brave.

Amid these closing scenes she unconsciously impressed all who saw her with her courage and sanguine temper, when opposite feelings might be expected. She was neither stern nor sad, though she had toiled constantly, and endured so much with no reward except the gratitude of the soldiers; and the consciousness that she had performed a part, which had not been ineffectual in helping to restore the Union to its pristine glory.

While preparations were being made to drive the Confederates even from .the " last ditch " which they had vaunted to hold in spite of Providence, the great men of the nation were conferring with each other upon the momentous questions of the hour. Generals Grant and Sherman frequently met, and together visited the President, on board the *River Queen*, near City Point. In the elegant cabin of this steamer words were spoken that equaled those uttered in earlier centuries by the oracles of Egypt or Rome. Here President Lincoln's great and noble heart revealed itself to the whole republic. His advice and dictates were not only fraught with far-reaching wisdom, but

were so humane that something of a divine spirit
seemed interwoven with them.   From his position
upon the loftiest summit to which the statesman may
aspire, he used his influence to elevate the lowly;
and was not only generous to the rebellious people,
who had no alternative except to surrender upon his
own terms, but was to them most lenient and mag-
nanimous.

CHAPTER VII.

PRIL sunshine touched with glistening luster the budding foliage of the
woods, and crowned every ripple of
the rivers and streams with diamond
coronets. Nature smiled with the
usual beauty of spring-time, in spite
of the cruel ravages of war; and,
like her, Mrs. Bickerdyke appeared
as hopeful and energetic as if the
long years of strife and bloodshed had not made
her weary and worn.

The ancient dame would be rewarded for the sunshine she scattered by a bountiful harvest. But Mrs.
Bickerdyke's deeds of kindness would be recom-

(148)

pensed only with the friendship and gratitude of those whom she had comforted. The fruits of her labor were not material riches; and to her, victory offered no laurels and gold lace.

During this time, General Sheridan's famous cavalry had cut off all supplies from the city, of Richmond, where the larger part of the Confederate forces were stationed under the command of General Lee. On the 2d day of April, 1865, this impenetrable stronghold was evacuated during the night, which was made hideous by the lurid flames, kindled in the heart of the ill-fated city. General Grant had just carried the defensive works of Petersburg by a spirited assault, and upon the next day the United States soldiers entered this captured city and the smouldering ruins of Richmond.

The Rebellion lasted but a short time longer. All of the most powerful armies of the Union were converging towards the exhausted and discouraged Confederate veterans, who were reduced in numbers, and desperate for want of supplies. Though they resisted valiantly, fighting with fierce energy, and burning the bridges that spanned the Appomattox River, as they retreated toward North Carolina, their efforts were all in vain. General Sheridan, who had won such splendid laurels in the valley of the Shenandoah, rendered General Grant great assistance. By brilliant fighting, and rapid and vigorous movements, he succeeded in cutting off Lee's supplies, and capturing his half-demoralized divisions. The mighty army of the Potomac gained some new advantage over the

Confederates with each succeeding day, and the utter uselessness of a further struggle on their side soon became apparent.

Events crowded upon each other with startling rapidity. The sweet bells of Palm Sunday, ringing through the fresh spring atmosphere, sounded the knell of the Confederacy, that had long been tottering to its fall. Now this dream of a Southern empire, which had kindled the flame of selfish ambition in unnumbered bosoms, and cost a million of lives, dissolved like some ghostly fantasy.

Upon this day, the 9th of April, 1865, the iron-souled General Lee, who had fought with such inflexible energy and skill for the losing cause, surrendered his army to General Grant, our nation's greatest hero. They met in Appomattox Court House, where the terms of the surrender were discussed and settled. The news of this tremendous event was borne through the land on the wings of lightning, filling it with the greatest joy and excitement. Cities and towns were thronged with people, who expressed their feelings in prolonged shouts, and by the thunder of artillery, which reverberated over mountains and plains, awakening ceaseless echoes. At night the country vied with the starry hosts of heaven in the number of bonfires spangling it throughout. They blazed in every loyal city and town, and upon the farms and ranches even to the most remote, which had been reached by the grand tidings.

The civil war was regarded as at an end. No more would the dreadful bloodshed and devastation which

it had caused, continue to make home a place of deso-
lation, and fill the land with soldiers' graves. Yet the
nation's cup of bitterness had not been drained to the
dregs, until President Lincoln died at the hands of
an assassin, a martyr's death.

Where now were the bursts of delight that had
filled the air with music, and unfurled ten thousand
flags upon every breeze? The gorgeous stars and
stripes were lowered in mourning, and the black sign
of lamentation draped the whole United States, from
ocean to ocean. This sad event was truly an afflic-
tion to the entire republic; and the solemn beat of
muffled drums sounded in unison with the sorrow so
deeply and so widely felt in the hearts of the people·

While these important historical events were taking place, Mrs. Bickerdyke was still engaged in her
noble work.· Whether national joy or sorrow prevailed to awaken her patriotic feelings, there was always enough to keep her willing hands and heart engaged among the soldiers, who needed the care of
relatives and friends, from whom they were widely
separated.

Like a true veteran, she adapted herself to all
places with ease; and seemed undisturbed by any
change, being as much at home in a bare tent, or
in a deserted house, as in a hospital, well organized,
and supplied with sanitary stores. Her life was
eventful, and although not so full of excitement, it
resembled, in many particulars, that which she had
experienced at Corinth. All her wishes and opinions
were regarded with much consideration by the au-

thorities, and this greatly facilitated her power of doing good. Mounted upon a horse, which had been appropriated to her use, she was free to come and go anywhere within the Federal lines at pleasure. She might often be seen riding over the winding roads, or through the natural arbors of the woodlands, upon some bridle path. Now and then she returned the smiling salute of a soldier, as he passed loaded like an old-fashioned farmer with a basket of onions or eggs, or even with a lot of spring chickens, destined to broil over a bivouac fire.

The armies were ordered to move from their present quarters on the 14th of April. They had already begun to advance, with the expectation of laying waste the central or the western parts of the State, when General Johnston surrendered his army to General Sherman, and this decisive event ended the campaign of the Carolinas.

Thereupon the armies of General Sherman were ordered to Alexandria. Mrs. Bickerdyke followed them there, and joined the 15th Army Corps on her arrival, at the request of General Logan. Again she clasped the friendly hand of many a soldier whom she had known at Vicksburg and Lookout Mountain. They had traveled far since those great battles had been fought. General O. O. Howard had succeeded to the command of the Army of the Tennessee, after the death of the brave McPherson. He led these dauntless veterans from Atlanta over the hundreds of miles to the sea, and thence to North Carolina, all the way culling fresh laurels, ere the dew had ceased to sparkle upon those which had just been gathered. After the surrender of General Johnston, he was summoned to Washington to take charge of an important bureau, and from that time the Army of the Tennessee was commanded by General Logan.

When peace was declared, the immense armies of General Sherman, in the vicinity of Washington, numbered 65,000 men. For months, this legion had subsisted principally upon the rebellious South; but now the cessation of hostilities suddenly checked this source of supplies. The Government had not yet been able to provide sufficient food for them, and they became short of rations. These strong, active men, living entirely in the open air, would miss keenly a meal at any time, and after spirited marches the lack of sufficient food made them exceedingly uncomfortable and dissatisfied. Their distress was greatly increased, because they could not learn how soon they were to be relieved from this predicament. The 15th Army Corps reached Alexandria on the 19th of April, a beautiful spring Sabbath; and there the men soon built cheerful campfires, and pitched their tents, or made themselves comfortable in deserted houses. The smoke curled up in the sunshine, and beds of glowing coals shone red through the flames. But where could be found anything to broil, or roast in the whole encampment?

Mrs. Bickerdyke appreciated fully the situation, and, as usual, was equal to the emergency. After several unavailing efforts to procure the desired provisions from the proper sources, she sent a telegram to the

Rev. Dr. Bellows, of New York, explaining to him their situation.

At the time of its receipt he was in the pulpit of his church, and before him his large congregation was assembled, with the usual hush of peace that renders so impressive and e 'ifying the hour of divine worship. During a pause in his sermon a messenger came up the aisle and quietly gave him a small envelope which contained the simple words of Mrs. Bickerdyke, appealing earnestly on behalf of the soldiers for food.

Dr. Bellows read it to his audience, and they quick'y responded to the call. A train was chartered immediately, and by four o'clock in the afternoon it was ready to start with an abundant supply of all that was needed to satisfy the hungry boys in blue. The telegram which heralded its arrival soon became known to the soldiers, and the news of what Mother Bickerdyke had done thrilled the whole encampment. Animation and happy expectations beamed from every sun-bronzed countenance; and the spirit of merriment prevailed, which found a climax when the provisions arrived, in national airs and grand old hymn tunes played by the bands, and many ringing cheers.

On Monday there was plenty, and as their delightful meals were discussed, Mrs. Bickerdyke was thanked and praised until her cheeks flushed and her eyes sparkled with pleasure. This wave of popularity was still bearing to l er feet new tributes of the general favor in which she was held, when the army was ordered to Washington for the grand review. The signal to march found the soldiers even more alert than usual. Their steps were as light and firm and their hearts beat as high with hope, as though the music of fife and drum had a power to inspire them like that which pealed from the shell of Orpheus. Every train steaming toward the capital bore friends and loved ones on the way to meet them there; and such pleasant anticipations filled every mind that the march of twelve miles from Alexandria was like going to a festival. Mrs. Bickerdyke, mounted upon her glossy saddle horse, accompanied them. She wore her usual simple dress, which, at this warm season, was of calico; and her clear eyes and serene countenance looked out from the depths of a comfortable sunbonnet. Her face was as fair, and free from freckle or tan, as though she had never seen the brawny veterans who esteemed her so highly, nor toiled for them through the sunny weather of a Southern spring.

She crossed the Long Bridge in advance of the 15th Army Corps, and was met by the noted Dorothy Dix, and others, who welcomed her to the capital. This greeting to the soldiers' mother was indeed a triumph such as few women have ever merited or won.

The streets now looked blue with the uniforms of moving thousands, for the grand review of the Army of the Potomac was now taking place. Onward those glorious legions were sweeping, while the wise and brave of the land scanned them with admiration, and the world rejoiced. General Grant, their great leader, whose star of fame now shone in the zenith of glory, looked calmly upon the superb pageant; and those who had seen him at Shiloh and Vicksburg thought his expression as unperturbed then, amid those scenes of fury and bloodshed, as it was now, beholding the victorious forces that moved in glittering columns through avenues of light and music.

That night the soldiers bivouacked in the streets of Washington, which gleamed far out into the suburbs with their myriad camp-fires. The 24th of April dawned clear and lovely. Stately trees held aloft their misty mantles of young leaves, and the air was fragrant with early flowers. The signal gun was fired at nine o'clock, and immediately the thoroughfares were filled with people in holiday attire. Dense masses of men, women, and children, all with glad, eager faces, stood in gardens and upon the streets, nearly obstructing the way.

General Sherman with his staff, accompanied by General Howard, all mounted upon their handsome chargers, rode slowly down Pennsylvania Avenue, followed by General Logan and the 15th Army Corps. Then came the other famous corps which had marched through Georgia to the sea, and swept the Carolinas like a storm. The columns, bright with blue and gold, moved in perfect concert. Above their heads a forest of polished bayonets caught the sunbeams, making a galaxy of light, which was relieved at intervals by their gorgeous silken flags that had been tattered and powder-stained in battle, and which were now garlanded with flowers.

Sharp swords flashed in the light, as the illustrious generals, who had just inscribed their names upon their country's history, saluted the president in true military style, as they passed the reviewing stand. Thousands of spectators scrutinized for hours the magnificent army of 65,000 veterans marching by them· They were fascinated with the spectacle of those vast walls of strength, bright with the trappings that graced the exultant hour of triumph. Gold fringes quivered from the epaulets of distinguished men, mounted upon war steeds, prancing and champing their silver bits. Then came the soldiers who had faced the flaming cannon, and the leaden hail of musketry. For ·these, cheer after cheer went up, while some, missing from the ranks the brave men who had fallen, dropped for them a tear.

There were enlivening features, the baggage trains being represented by ambulances, followed by pack-mules, loaded with such things as hams, and festooned with carrot tops and onions, or perhaps bags of corn and cackling poultry formed the pack. Cattle lowed, as they followed in the train, and among them were the glossy milch cows, distinguished for having had their horns so brightly polished by the "jovial boys," in honor of Mother Bickerdyke. Negro women, leading their children, who in turn led goats, ornamented with jingling bells, added variety. The corps of black pioneers at the heads of the divisions, carrying their axes and spades, marched in creditable style. The whole grand review was remarkable for the perfect discipline of the soldiers, and for the beauty and strength of every detail, making it one of the greatest pageants ever beheld in America.

During the weeks that followed this memorable day, the greater part of the army was disbanded. Still thousands remained, and among these Mrs. Bickerdyke found ample work, so she stayed in the vicinity, distributing stores and caring for the sick, just as she had been doing all though the spring. The popularity she had gained called forth much notice, from which she shrank with extreme modesty; and yet all of it she could not escape. She was treated with marked distinction on numerous occasions.

The calico dress and sunbonnet which she had worn upon her arrival, were sold for $100, and preserved as relics of the Rebellion. This sum of money melted from her hands almost in a day, for the "boys" needed so many things that she delighted to supply. General O. O. Howard remembers her at this time, and says, " I always heard her called, when spoken of, Mother Bickerdyke, the soldiers' friend. She was a woman of great energy of character, and successful in procuring from the people large supplies for the relief of the sick and wounded. Her labors were spoken of everywhere with kind words of praise and thankfulness."

The work which Mrs. Bickerdyke did among the soldiers here, all through the golden days of June, was as much needed and as highly appreciated as any during the whole period of civil strife. She went about the camps in a huge army wagon, loaded with stores of all kinds; and distributed with her own hands great bales of clean linen, and countless pounds of dainty eatables for those who were suffering from sickness or exhaustion.

It was her greatest pleasure to enter some tent, where languished a poor weary boy, so disheartened and fatigued by the recent hardships of war that life itself was a burden, and there diffuse the sparkling animation of her own lively and hopeful disposition. She always brought some pleasing gift—perhaps a glass of jelly, clear as a topaz, or a soft pillow, and some fresh white towels. These were given with a native grace and smile, which made them thrice welcome.

Here in sight of the capitol gleaming like a palace of marble over the roofs of the city, in which the beauty and wealth and wisdom of the whole nation concentrated, Mrs. Bickerdyke wore as simple a dress, and every action was as modest and unselfish, as when she had labored so earnestly, where roared the artillery for a hundred days at the fall of Georgia's citadel. What to her were the pomp and pleasures enjoyed in yonder banquet halls? She lived in a different world. In the valley of humility she saw true heroes—the brave self-sacrificing soldiers, who had given their all for the Union—poor and neglected in sickness, and far from friends and home. It seemed as though a kind Providence had implanted in her heart so much kindness, and such broad sympathies, that she might take the place of those mothers who yearned anxiously for their absent sons.

As the summer advanced, large numbers of soldiers

left the fair city of Washington, and when General Logan ordered his army to different scenes, he requested Mrs. Bickerdyke to remain with them. For months she traveled through the South and West, engaged in such occupations as have hitherto been described; for though the battles were ended, and once more national peace began to revive prosperity, the loss of which had affected the whole contin nt, thousands of men had become disabled or unfit for civil occupations. The great military hospitals were crowded with them, and many of the cities were filled with discharged soldiers, who could find no suitable employment. Through lingering weeks Mrs. Bickerdyke was familiarly seen in the haunts of pain, and wherever distress or sickness were found. Her large sense of right and justice was frequently offended by the neglect of men, who, though brought to poverty and with no ambition, she knew had been reduced to their present state through one of the most sublime sentiments—that of patriotism.

In Chicago she did a noble deed for them. Large numbers of soldiers had gathered there, and were unable to obtain work. Our country grants special privileges to men who have served in the army, when they wish to take up public lands, and Mrs. Bickerdyke was active in causing a vast number of veterans in Chicago to settle the promising prairies of Kansas, which then were uncultivated wilds. These men were well fitted for the lives of frontiersmen, having acquired a taste for adventure, and being accustomed to active labor in the open air.

Being encouraged to industry and enterprise, they succeeded admirably in their attempts, and now their homes, in the midst of waving grain fields, present the most charming pictures of domestic usefulness and comfort.

Mrs. Bickerdyke often receives letters from those who were " her boys," in the by-gone days of the Rebellion, telling her of contented and happy lives here, surrounded by all that renders existence delightful. Photographs are sent of fair and dimpled children, who are the treasures and ornaments of the happy firesides so glowingly described; and upon every leaf of those friendly missives, are words of gratitude for what Mother Bickerdyke has enabled them to enjoy.

The days of life's decline find her still employed with her chosen tasks. For nearly ten years she has lived chiefly in San Francisco, and though her circumstances have been straitened, compelling her many times to seek employment as a nurse, in order that she might maintain herself, she has done much in securing richly-deserved pensions for soldiers who have been seriously maimed in the late war. She has countless letters from them, asking for a word of remembrance, or other aid; and in their behalf she has journeyed several times to Washington, where her efforts were of great value to them.

Upon one occasion, as she was returning from the capital, she was met at Topeka by several hundred soldiers, who had known her during the war, or at Chicago afterwards. The cars stopped but a short time yet her hand was taken in the frank clasp of

11

so many friends, that she was unable to offer it longer; and blessings were showered upon the "dear old mother of the soldiers." When the train was about to start, hearty cheers for the "general" filled the air, recalling the old days of youthful enthusiasm and patriotic fervor.

This incident is related by Mrs. William Spinning, wife of the young cavalryman mentioned in the third chapter. Since the war he became a minister of the gospel, and now has charge of a parish at the mission within a few blocks of Mrs. Bickerdyke's present home. Mr. Spinning brought his family to San Francisco quite recently, and as they were on the journey hither, they happened to be on the same train with Mrs. Bickerdyke. In the cozy parsonage at the quiet old mission, voices ring sweetly out in the music of childish glee; and here she is received with more than courteous warmth, her welcome being tinged with a sense of gratitude for her kindness long ago to the young soldier at Corinth.

Time, that wizard, who is constantly followed by changes, often permits them to come stealing in his footsteps so insidiously that a retrospective glance is startling. Hundreds of young volunteers who joined the army in 1861, and in the dark years that followed, dwell here upon the calm Pacific shores,

> Where opal waves
>   Come softly beating from the west,
> Bearing like crowns the pearly sprays
>   That glisten on each rounded crest.
>
> They have laved the Orient shore that lies
>   'Neath summer suns that ne'er retreat,
> And yet they are nearer Paradise,
>   When here at California's feet.

Some also who have won laurels upon those crimsoned fields of the Rebellion grace the city with their presence. General Stoneman, governor of this State, is often seen at reviews and parades of the National Guard; and thus he calls to mind his inestimable services to the Union, during the spring of 1865, when he led his cavalry corps across the mountains of Tennessee on his famous raid through the South.

General O. O. Howard, now in command of the Military Division of the Pacific, has his headquarters at Fort Mason, or Black Point, as it is usually called, where his home is surrounded by gardens of perpetual flowers, and looks across the water upon fort-crowned Alcatraz, that sets like a jewel upon the bosom of the bay. Northward, the purple heights of Mount Tamalpais rise among the green hills of Marin County, from which Angel Island, with its smooth outlines, is separated by a narrow channel. Buildings cluster upon the shores; and fine ferry-boats and queenly ships breast the tranquil waters, while trim yachts are lightly wafted about, giving a sense of life and action to the beautiful view.

In the evening, the sunset gun is fired from the terraced slopes of Alcatraz; and as the dusk deepens into night, the flashing light from the beacon on the battlements at Foit Point tells to mariners, with the constancy of the North Star, where may be found the Golden Gate. When all surrounding objects are obscured by volumes of fog, which sometimes creep in from the sea, the deep tones of the sirene do this duty.

The Presidio of San Francisco was established as a

military post to protect the first missionaries, and was occupied by Spanish and Mexican troops, until the year 1847, when it passed under the dominion of the United States. Its history is intimately connected with the Mission Dolores, from which a single road wound across the hills. when those between it and the beach, upon which the city of San Francisco now rests, was mantled only with primeval shrubbery and wild verdure.

The National Cemetery is in the Government Reservation, adjoining the Presidio, and here, departed soldiers sleep. Among them, General Irwin McDowell is laid to rest. Beneath the ivy and cedars that flourish in the Odd Fellows' Cemetery, slumber many soldiers, and General Miller, the late United States Senator, is interred among those tablet covered eminences.

Colonel Edward D. Baker reposes,

Where marble spires crown the hills
Within the Golden Gate,
The breeze from the Pacific thrills
Through trees that seem to wait

For night to cover them with dew
Which they may shed like tears,
Above the men who wore the blue,
And fell in other years.

The mournful march and minute guns
Sound on Memorial Day,
When memory culls for those brave sons
The opening gems of May.

In Laurel Hill a soldier sleeps,
One of illustrious name,
Whose services our history keeps
Upon the page of fame.

'Twas he who led the ranks of blue,
Upon that fatal day
At Ball's Bluff, and who never knew
The terror of dismay.

He fell upon that gory field,
And now he slumbers here.
Unto his honored tomb we yield
Fair blossoms, with a tear

That wells where sorrow's fountain leaps,
And yet 'tis half of pride,
That in our fair young land now sleeps
One who so bravely died.

At Arlington Heights, near the city of Washington, thousands of green hillocks billow the peaceful slopes, and beneath them an army slumbers. One evening a stranger came through the dusk, and, after scanning with earnest eyes a number of the headstones, knelt beside a grave and bedewed it with tears. Neither father, brother, nor son slumber there; yet it was one united to him by ties as strong. It was his friend—a friend who had died for him. When he was drafted into the army, and was about to be compelled to leave an invalid wife and four helpless little children, two of them still in infancy, a noble young man who had no such domestic ties, volunteered to take his place. This brave soldier marched away in the beauty and promise of youth, and fell in battle. He was so fortunate as to be buried in a grave on these hallowed slopes, and with each returning Memorial day, fresh blossoms are left upon the sacred mound by th · friend for whom he died.

Such inci ents were not rare during those terrible years of the Rebellion, and they are deeds to which we may look up with feelings of adoration, since they prove the existence of something divine in the human heart.

This scene suggests a simile—Mother Bickerdyke kneeling upon the gory fields to bind up wounds, watching at midnight in dreary hospital wards, smoothing the hot pillows of those who rave in the delirium of fever, and hurrying through the icy gales of winter to frail tents, with life-saving potions, all are typical of what the mothers of those soldiers yearned to do, and would nave done had it been possible. In their place Mrs. Bickerdyke visited those scenes, and in their stead toiled through those long and sorrowful years.

She deserves from them, not a wreath of fading flowers, but the true and earnest friendship of sisters. Every heart that has glowed with a mother's love must thrill with sympathy for this exalted mother, while those whose sons were soldiers cannot choose but pay to her the tribute of soul-felt gratitude.

The esteem and favor in which she is held by the officers and rank and file of the United States army have been illustrated by incidents in the preceding pages. These sentiments are richly merited, having been won by her womanly tenderness, her noble intellect, and exalted character. The services which she has rendered to our country cannot be estimated, though they are so widely attested by the name that covers her with honor and fame. She is a heroine in the eyes of thousands, and as long as warm life-blood beats in the hearts of those who fought in the great Western army, there will always be arms to protect and lips to praise Mrs. Bickerdyke, the soldier's mother, and the soldier's friend.

www.ingramcontent.com/pod-product-compliance
Lightning Source LLC
Chambersburg PA
CBHW021109020726
47500CB00003B/671